THE SENSIBLE NECKTIE
and other stories of Sherlock Holmes

Peter K. Andersson

Paperback ISBN 978-1-78092-815-9
ePub ISBN 978-1-78092-816-6
PDF ISBN 978-1-78092-817-3

Published in the UK by MX Publishing
335 Princess Park Manor, Royal Drive,
London, N11 3GX
www.mxpublishing.co.uk

Cover design by www.staunch.com

Contents

The Adventure of the Sensible Necktie

Though we live in an age when exposure to the public gaze is increasingly dismissed as commercial greed, I take up my pen once more to chronicle some further exploits of my friend Sherlock Holmes, spurred not by the promise of a juicy advance from my publisher – there is none – but by the growing inclination towards nostalgia that overcomes a man who sees the world changing beyond recognition around him. In such a situation it is the hunger for memories and the – albeit illusory – comfort of the world of one's younger days, not for profit, that makes one want to sit down and reminisce. The reveries awaken recollections of numerous cases that I should have committed to the written record long ago, but which were sidetracked in preference of more scandalous adventures. Now that I am an older man, it is not the melodramatic escapades that I find interesting – those that my younger self was more prone to recount – but the cases that had the nature of placid mind exercises or which were characterised by their eccentricities rather than their connections to sensational crimes. One such affair was the baffling case of Mr Cyrus Thicknesse of Belsize Park, which took place in the early days of April 1898.

As I came down to breakfast one morning, I noticed a cabinet photograph placed up against the clock on our mantelpiece. It was a portrait of an ordinary and decent-looking man, slim and tall, with a shaved face and a stern expression, dressed neatly in a black suit and tie, posing elegantly with his hand upon the habitual plaster Roman column. He was not familiar to me, and I drew Holmes' attention towards it when he emerged from his bedroom, wiping superfluous shaving cream from his cheeks.

"Oh, that," he said, as if he had forgotten all about it. "It came this morning. There was a note with it. You will find it on the table, next to the teapot."

I sauntered over and seated myself before the breakfast tray, pouring myself a cup of Darjeeling while I glanced through the message.

"Dear Mr Holmes," I read, "please find enclosed the likeness of my brother, Mr Cyrus Thicknesse, whose disappearance took place a month ago, the details of which you will surely have read about in the papers. Since that time there have been developments which I cannot make head or tail of, and which I should like to discuss with you at the earliest possible moment. I will call upon you at eleven today. Yours sincerely, Mr Ellis Thicknesse."

Holmes was standing by the fire, the photograph now in his hand.

"The papers did make quite a big affair of Thicknesse's disappearance. He was a common City clerk, commuting punctually every day between his office and his home in Belsize Park. One Tuesday morning, however, he did not show up at his work, and a police inquiry was initiated. It transpired that he left his flat that morning as usual, witnessed by his landlady, but that instead of going to the City he took a train into the country. He was seen boarding the morning train from Paddington to Oxford, and a man who sat opposite him during the entire journey claimed that he went at least as far as Goring and Streatley, where the witness disembarked. However, on the next station in the village of Chilton Gifford, where the train was held for a few minutes due to a problem with the points, the station-master walked through it, finding that there were only three passengers in the entire sequence of carriages: an old woman with a child and a one-legged retired soldier. The only other mysterious thing was a curtain that had been stuck halfway down in one of the compartments."

"Doesn't sound too mystifying," I remarked. "The man probably jumped out of the train when it was standing still, before the station-master had had time to walk through it."

"Yes, only there was a porter on the platform who had clear sight of the train from one side, and on the other is a row of terraced houses, the backyards of which would have to have been crossed in full sight of numerous people. Mr Thicknesse was never seen by anyone, and his whereabouts have not been established since then."

"To me, it is obvious that the man who sat opposite him is lying in his statement," I said, helping myself to some more scrambled eggs. "He probably did away with him."

"A stranger he has never seen before? We would have trouble establishing a motive, Watson."

"Well, I am sure his brother will provide us with the necessary missing pieces of the puzzle. Why do you think he has contacted you?"

"Of that we can only guess. What intrigues me more is the reason why he should send me the man's photograph."

"To help us in our inquiries?"

"Or to underline a point he wishes to make. You are a keen observer of human nature, Watson. What do you make of the man?"

He tossed down the portrait on the table beside me. I looked at it carefully, but I only saw the aspects that came across in hundreds of similar photographs – the pose minutely arranged by the photographer, the attempt at conveying an air of dignity and delicateness, and the archetypal qualities of the painted background and the column on which he was leaning.

"If you have seen one, you have seen them all, Holmes. Pictures like that say very little about the people in them."

"Yes, having been exposed to numerous portraits of identical design we tend to become quite blind to whatever individualities they may contain. But if I were to say to you that the man in the picture is an obsessive pedant, that he has at one time worked as a schoolmaster and that there is a broken engagement in his past?"

"Then I would reply that you are a bounder."

Holmes chuckled secretively, and started pacing the room like a professor interrogating his students.

"His teaching days are present in the picture in the form of the pendant on the watch-chain. I took the time to study it under an eyeglass, and managed to identify it as the emblem of the National Schoolmaster's Association. Since we know that the man works as a City clerk, this must be a relic of a past affinity. In his breast pocket is a white handkerchief, much like the handkerchief found in thousands of similar breast pockets on thousands of similar middle-class men in this country. Or so most people would think, not paying any particular attention to it. But one must never falter in one's suspicion of the ordinary, Watson, and I placed my eyeglass over this detail as well. Do you notice the uneven nature of the upper edge of the handkerchief? When you look closely, you will see that this is not due to it being frayed. What a quick glance perceives as the worn edge of a gentleman's handkerchief is in fact the lace edge of a lady's handkerchief! So here, all of a sudden, we have a lover's keepsake, worn close to the heart, presumably on a daily basis, but no other evidence of courtship in this man's life. In fact, it is well known that he was a bachelor."

"But steady on a minute there, Holmes," I protested. "How can you be so sure that he has not fallen in love recently, and is actually courting a young lady, albeit in secret?"

"Because if you look at this handkerchief, you will notice that it is of a fashion that was popular at least five years ago, and nowadays is seen as quite an outdated accessory. No, no, this was most certainly given to him several years ago, in which case it was the sign of serious affection, which has since then vanished."

"I suppose you may be right. But what of his pedantry?"

"Come, Watson, the whole appearance of the man is littered with the signs. Buttons buttoned, collar unwrinkled, tie straight. Not to mention his hair!" Holmes reached for his magnifying glass and looked closely at the photo. "Yes, Circassian Cream pomade, unless I am very much mistaken. The way it is parted down the middle, in a line that could be measured with a ruler, strongly suggests a most meticulous mind. A pedant."

Holmes handed me the picture and I looked at it.

"And what are we to make of that?"

"We are to make very little of that until our visitor has arrived. It is tempting to jump to conclusions, but in my vocation that is a deadly sin, for it invariably clouds one's judgement."

Two hours later, we were both dressed and waited eagerly for our announced client to arrive. When he did so, we were surprised to encounter the complete opposite of the man we had seen in the cabinet photograph. Mr Ellis Thicknesse was a heavyset and frolicsome man, who met us with a hearty smile in spite of the sadness of his purpose in visiting us. He was a younger man than the serious official staring out from the photograph, but his eyes shone with a confidence and composure that his elder brother appeared to lack.

Holmes and I bid him good morning and we seated ourselves in the armchairs while our visitor composed his thoughts.

"I come to you to present you with some developments in the case of my poor brother, which surely transforms it from a mystery into something much stranger. As I am certain you know, my brother vanished without a trace from the 8.15 train to Oxford, and despite exhaustive efforts by the police, which included knocking on every door within a three-mile radius of the station at Chilton Gifford, no clues have been found that could lead to a solution. I am myself an independent businessman, selling tools to workshops, and I have a number of regular customers in the area surrounding London. Thus it was that I happened to be travelling on the exact same line only two days ago, bound for a small horseshoe manufacturing workshop in Woodstock. I had some misgivings about going along that route so soon after the incident, but I felt no great unease until I was approaching Goring. And perhaps it was my mind playing tricks on me, perhaps my head was so full of my dear brother's image, but when the train pulled up at Chilton Gifford Station, who was there on the platform but he, standing by the wall of the station building for a few seconds before walking away round the corner and disappearing from view! I was completely flabbergasted, but just then I heard the whistle announcing our departure, and I had to think fast. Quickly, I grabbed my bag and jumped out of the carriage, seconds before it started moving. There was no doubt in my mind that the man I had seen was my brother, even though there was something different about him. I hurried across the platform to the corner of the building where he had walked, and I found myself standing on a deserted gravelly country road without an inkling of what I would do next or where my brother could have got to. Feverishly, I rummaged around the immediate area, trying to unearth some traces, but all I could find was a sleepy and unattractive village, created for the commuters who are unable to afford a home in the London suburbs.

"Instead of continuing a drawn-out and fruitless search on my own, I contacted the police, who sent a sergeant and a constable. They did not seem particularly interested in the case, though, as they frequently reminded me that they had already scoured the area in search of traces. As we wandered around the village, their irritation grew, and eventually they had to get back to Oxford, implying that they believed my sighting to be the result of overexertion. I could not drive myself to leave the village, however, now that I was certain that Cyrus was near, and so I decided to put up for the night at the local inn. Since Cyrus' disappearance, I have taken to carrying his photograph about with me, and that evening I showed it to everyone who came into the taproom. I was unable to evoke any positive response, however, and I went to bed dissatisfied and confused by the day's experiences.

"The next morning, I went back to London, bent on doing something constructive instead of letting this run out into the sand. I conferred with my wife, whose sister – a Miss Rose Dobson – you were helpful to a few years ago and who has spoken highly of you since then. My wife thus suggested I lay the matter before you, and I thought the notion was a capital one. Now here I am."

Holmes nodded pensively from the depths of his armchair.

"Dobson, Dobson – yes, I seem to recall the case, something to do with a poison-pen letter, I believe. But your case leaves little room for meditation, Mr Thicknesse.

Disappearing not once but twice may be considered strange of your brother, but the second disappearance does not annul the first one. In cases such as this one must, I fear, pose a very difficult question to the next of kin: Is there any possibility that your brother does not wish to be found?"

Mr Thicknesse squinted at Holmes. "I appreciate your reasons for asking the question, but I must reply in the negative. Cyrus led a contented life. He was quite uninterested in the fair sex, and he loved the routinised existence that his office work allowed him to lead. In his younger years, he endeavoured to become a schoolmaster, but his pedantic lifestyle made this occupation unbearable for him and he was compelled to abandon it, in defiance of his ambitions."

Holmes could not avoid shooting me a victorious glance. "But you said," he continued, "there was something different about your brother when you saw him on the platform."

"Yes, there certainly was. At first, I could not quite put my finger on it, but when I had gone over the moment in my mind afterwards, I realised what it was. It was his necktie."

"His necktie?"

"Yes. He was wearing a bright green necktie with maroon dots."

"And your brother does not own such a tie?"

"Mr Holmes, my brother would not be seen dead in such a tie! If you knew him as I did, you would understand that he had very clear conceptions of his appearance, and his strict and meticulous nature was expressed through these conceptions. He always wore black or grey suits together with black or grey neckties, and anything else jarred glaringly with his personality. He would never wear a tie of such a bright and vulgar colour! His attire was always so decent and sensible. That is why I sent his photograph ahead to you, so that you could see with your own eyes the solidity and sobriety of his nature."

"Was he wearing anything else that was conspicuous?"

"No. From what I remember, he wore a dark suit, which perhaps is why the tie broke off so obviously."

Holmes smiled, then smacked his lips as if he was tasting an expensive wine. "Mr Thicknesse, your case is most intriguing, but my instincts tell me that immediate measures are of necessity. I believe we should go to Chilton Gifford before the trail grows cold."

The village of Chilton Gifford lay in the centre of a shallow dale, surrounded by an area of thick woodlands unusual for that part of Oxfordshire. As we stepped from the train onto the platform, I was struck by how provincial and small the place seemed. No other people stepped on or off the train, and the stationmaster stood idly by as we paced the length of the platform. Ellis Thicknesse showed us the place where he had seen his brother standing before walking away. Holmes undertook a lengthy examination of the ground before looking up and turning to us.

Mr Thicknesse could not contain his giddiness. "I have been going over it in my mind, time and time again," he said. "Why would he be standing here in the first place. Was he waiting for someone? Did he intend to board the train, then changed his mind? Or was his business here something else, unrelated to the railway?"

"Yes, all very pertinent questions," said Holmes, "although it is pointless to be asking them at the moment because we have nothing to help us answer them. They are all secondary to the only question we should be trying to find an answer to at the moment: Why did he wear such a brightly-coloured tie?"

"But that is an even more impossible question, Holmes!" I protested.

"Is it? Perhaps. But it arouses thought-provoking speculations, does it not?"

"Yes, I suppose so. You mean that he became bored with his own drab existence and longed for an escape, so he put on a tie that was as far from his usual self as he could imagine and took the first train out of London?"

"Precisely."

"Do you believe that is what happened?"

"Preposterous!" Mr Thicknesse exclaimed. "My brother was not the main character in a novel of romance. Not all sensible and restrained gentlemen are suppressed dreamers, you know!"

"I have no doubt in my mind," said Holmes, "that the explanation that Watson has just provided us with is as far from the truth as one can get. But sometimes the opposite of the truth may point us in the direction of the truth itself. If Cyrus Thicknesse was so far from the dreamer that you say, then he would not take a train out of London, breaking his meticulous routine, without a very good reason, and most likely against his own will."

"I could have told you that," said Mr Thicknesse.

"Indeed," said Holmes, "but what it points to is two things. Firstly, that the green necktie you saw your brother wearing was not his own, and secondly, that what we are looking for is, most likely, a letter."

"You mean a letter that summoned him to Chilton Gifford?"

"If that was his destination."

"But should we not search for that letter in his home?" I asked.

"A letter of such importance that a pedant breaks his routine because of it, he would probably take with him on his journey. I believe this is a part of it."

Holmes held up a very small piece of paper, firmly clasped between his thumb and forefinger.

"Good God!" said Mr Thicknesse. "But how do you know that is my brother's letter?"

"That, my dear Mr Thicknesse, is still a matter of some debate, but the writing on it does tie together some loose ends."

Holmes gave it to our client, who held it up so that he and I could read it. The remains of two lines could be read:

e at the plat
ll be expla

"How strange," said Mr Thicknesse. "What do you think it could mean?"

"A not very wild guess," replied Holmes, "is that the full sentence reads 'Be' or 'Meet me at the platform and all will be explained', or something similar."

"You mean to say my brother had an appointment with someone here?"

"I mean just that. But the state of the letter suggests that he will not be coming back."

"Then we have come no further, have we?"

"I would not say that. Ask yourself this: if your brother was standing on the platform waiting for his appointment two days ago, why did he take a train here three weeks earlier?"

"Has he been waiting for three weeks?" I said.

"Or he has only recently been able to wait. Do you recall that when the stationmaster walked through the train here just after your brother's disappearance, he came across a jammed

15

curtain? It was a detail for which there was no explanation, and despite its trivial nature, I have suspected it to pertain to something important. You know how there are doors in every compartment of these trains that open directly onto the platform? If a passenger tried to pull down a curtain in one of these compartments, and the curtain was stuck but the door handle was loose, then the struggle to unjam the curtain might receive an unexpectedly dramatic conclusion."

"You mean he fell out trying to pull down the drape in his compartment?" I said.

"The sun was shining that morning, and the compartments on this part of the line face east."

"I cannot stand this!" cried Mr Thicknesse. "Will you tell us your suspicions, man? What happened to my brother?"

"I will explain on the way," said Holmes.

"What way?" said Mr Thicknesse.

Holmes asked us to wait, and then he walked up to the station house and knocked on the door of the station-master's office. A thin moustachioed man stepped out, and Holmes started speaking to him, remaining out of earshot. Mr Thicknesse and I waited patiently while they spoke, and after a few minutes, the station-master nodded and closed the door to his office. Holmes gestured at us to follow, and then the station-master led us along the platform. When he came to the end, however, we were surprised to find that he did not stop, but jumped down onto the ground and kept walking along the railway tracks. In this way we went along, our guide repeatedly instructing us to walk in a straight line and not go to near the tracks. A ten-minute walk took us to a small clearing in the woods that lined the tracks, and as we halted by the shelter of a few thick tree trunks, we saw a number of carriages parked in the centre of it. A thin string of smoke rose from a nearly extinguished fire in the middle, and we could hear the sound of rumbling and chatting from within some of the vehicles. Holmes patted the station-master on the shoulder, thanking him for his help, and then he stepped out into the clearing without hesitation. The rest of us followed him warily. We were not three paces from the edge of the trees when a man and a woman emerged from behind one of the carriages and looked at us with suspicious glances. Holmes spoke a few words in a foreign tongue I had no idea he was acquainted with. The woman replied curtly before vanishing once more behind the carriage. Not ten seconds later, she reappeared in the company of a man. Our client's reaction informed us promptly of his identity.

"Cyrus!"

The man squinted for a while, his face betraying no emotions.

"Ellis," he replied.

Mr Thicknesse stepped up to his brother, paused for a moment, then embraced him. It was a most moving scene, and Holmes and I stood by, allowing the revelation to sink in.

"How could you possibly know, Mr Holmes?" Ellis Thicknesse said in a broken voice while still clinging to his brother.

"I inferred that the only likely solution was that Mr Cyrus Thicknesse had somehow lost his memory. When I coupled the mystery of the jammed curtain with the lack of a sensible necktie, the conclusion that he had fallen off the train while trying to pull down the curtain, then hitting his head causing temporary memory loss was close at hand."

We all looked down at Cyrus Thicknesse's shirtfront. Hanging down it was the bright green spotted tie that his brother had described.

"Where on earth did you get this tie, Cyrus?"

"Ghastly, isn't it? But my own was torn when I fell from the train, and one cannot go without a tie, can one? These people, who took care of me when they found me senseless by the railway track, kindly lent me this one."

"Your description of the tie," said Holmes to our client, "indicated to me that gypsies fitted into this affair at some end. Watson and I were once involved in a case concerning just such a 'speckled band'," he added, and winked at me.

"Yes," said the station-master, "they have been camped here a few months now. I suppose it is a bit irregular, but they do no 'arm, do they, so who am I to tell 'em off?"

"They have been very kind," Cyrus Thicknesse agreed. "My memory started to come back gradually about a week ago. I remembered the train, trying to pull down that damned curtain and loosing my footing, falling on the door. But why had I been on the train in the first place? The gypsies had taken care of my suit, and I had the idea to search its pockets. I found a letter. It was from a woman named Ursula Prentiss. The name meant nothing to me at first, but slowly my memories of long ago were awakened. She was betrothed to me when I was a young man, but we were ill-matched, the result of an agreement by our parents. Eventually, we managed to break off the engagement and parted as friends. Her parting gift – a lace handkerchief – I have worn in my breast pocket to this day as a memento of her decent and sensible nature. Now, suddenly, she wrote to me saying that she needed my help. Her parents were once more trying to force her into marriage, not being able to accept that she wishes to live as a free woman. She wanted me to come to Chilton Gifford, where her parents live, and try to persuade them to desist. We were supposed to meet at the station and go to their house together. When I realised that I had missed the appointment, I was distraught and went there to see if she had left a message for me. She had not, and I could do nothing but keep waiting, as my memory was still patchy. I could not remember where I lived or where I worked, and so I could not return. All I could do was go to the station every day and wait for Ursula. Of course, it was futile. Finally, I realised that all was lost and tore up her message. It was not until now, when I saw you, Ellis, that the last pieces of my memory came back to me. Good God. I must return to London. What an uproar there must be at the office! I am only too glad my colleagues are not here to see me like this. We must get back to London, so that I can contact Ursula. Maybe it is not too late yet!"

And thus was the tale of one of the most chivalrous and dutiful men of my acquaintance. I was almost ashamed at how easily I had assumed that this pedantic man had succumbed to feelings of romance. The reality of it was that he had remained himself, more staunchly than any man I had encountered, and that he had endeavoured to save a woman who wished only the freedom to live like he did. How curious that two so similar people had been matched, only to see that they were so similar they could not possibly marry.

We took Cyrus Thicknesse with us after he had profoundly thanked his gypsy benefactors, and took the first train back to London. He was safely brought to his Belsize Park flat, where the first order was to put on a decent necktie. Holmes and I went back to Baker Street, but learned already the next day that he had been able to contact his former fiancée, whose engagement had not yet been initiated. We were ensured that both Cyrus and Ellis Thicknesse would work to prevent it from being so.

"A most admirable gentleman, Mr Cyrus Thicknesse," said Holmes as he reclined into his armchair. "His consistency should be a model for us all."

"It is like you to sing the praises of a man who puts reason before emotions," I commented.

"Call me predictable, my dear friend, but I sometimes think that it is the rational and unromantic people who bequeath to this world the real romance, when the starry-eyed only produce clouds that dissolve at the slightest puff."

A Patch of Mist

In the final weeks of November of the year 1901, the amount of work at my practice had piled up following a lengthy visit to Scotland attending a medical conference, and when the level of engagement started to dwindle, I suddenly found myself with some free time on my hands. It was in periods such as this that I was reminded of my old friend Sherlock Holmes, whom I had seen very little of for some months, and so, one morning in early December, I decided to pay him a long-postponed visit. The weather was unusually mild for the season, and I walked to our old lodgings in Baker Street with my overcoat unbuttoned and my wool scarf sticking out of my coat pocket. It was a bustling, busy day and I was pleased to be able to enjoy the streetlife of the metropolis without the sensation of duty or hurry pervading my mind. Mrs Hudson appeared delighted to see me, and her questions about my current life were so numerous that it was a full twenty minutes before I got round to climbing the stairs to the old sitting room.

The state of the room, which always transformed into a welcoming and cosy place in my memory when I had been away from it for some time, was enough to give me a start as I opened the door. All over the floor were scattered the pages of torn and trampled old newspapers; the breakfast table, beside which I had spent so many soothing hours, had been overtaken by an intricate chemical experiment involving a complex series of test tubes and Bunsen burners, and on Holmes' old desk by the bay windows lay half a dozen large folios opened on top of each other. In the midst of all this, in front of the roaring fire, stood Holmes, his pipe clenched between his teeth and his hands holding up a newspaper so close to his face that the glow from the pipe was in serious danger of setting fire to it.

"Is that you, Watson?" he said from behind the periodical. "Help yourself to a cigar. I will be with you shortly."

I took a cigar from the usual place, and seated myself in the sofa before the fire. I could hear Holmes make a dismissive sound and then he closed the newspaper and threw it over his shoulder, the same way as he must have with all the others.

"Watson, my dear chap," he said, extending his arms in a hospitable gesture. "So nice to see you after so long. Have a cigar, oh did I already—? So sorry, well things have been in a bit of a disarray here for the past few days."

He sat down in the armchair opposite me. He looked tired and overworked, but his face glowed with the lustre and energy that a constant supply of rewarding mental stimulation generally infused in him.

"You seem to be busy?" I said.

"I have been tremendously busy recently. As I have no doubt you have too. As a matter of fact, I read all about your success in Edinburgh. Well deserved, Watson, well deserved."

I confess I blushed.

"It is nothing, really. I suppose I have not the stamina of refusing to accept accolades that you have?"

"Tut, Watson. Some accolades are mere knick-knacks, but others are the fruits of hard labour."

"And what of your hard labour? Any fruits?"

"I cannot say I need to go hungry. But illustrious clients, such as those you may have read of in the papers, serve better as advertisements for my agency than as benefactors of its finances. They seem curiously aware of this themselves. My only compensation for my recent services to the Grand Duchess Constantia, for instance, was a silver candlestick that I immediately pawned. In fact, my recent work has to a large degree been about trading in various useless valuables for hard currency that will put food on my plate."

"From what I understand, these cases are seldom rich in challenging puzzles. I seem to recall an extremely trifling matter involving the Crown Princess of Hungary and a missing lapdog."

"I try not to be prejudiced at the outset, and treat every case with an equal degree of seriousness, but it is trying sometimes."

He relit his extinguished pipe and leaned his head back. Just then, the chemical experiment on the table behind me started to emit strange and ominous hissing sounds, and Holmes bolted from his seat to attend to it. He turned off the gas flames, and picked up one of the test tubes, into which a yellowish liquid had been dripping from a spout.

"Disaster," he stated placidly, before putting the tube down again and returning to his seat.

"You appear to be in the throes of a more demanding commission at the moment," I said.

"Hum! Yes, it is a case of some difficulty. One of my problems is that I lack a sparring partner to test my theories on, and not least someone to throw foolish theories at me from which I may be guided towards the truly inspired ones."

"I recognise that description."

"Oh, Watson! You are sorely missed in these quarters. My conductor of light. But now that you are here, perhaps you would be interested in hearing the details of the case upon which I have been consulted?"

"Naturally."

"You gladden me, dear friend. It is a problem of some complexity containing various possible loose ends to tug at. For the time being, I have become obsessed with matters of weather in connection with it, and by consulting the morning papers of the past few weeks, I have been trying to piece together the recent movements of high and low pressures across the English Channel. But I am getting ahead of myself, and seem to have picked up your old habit of telling a story the wrong way around. You must think that I have finally lost my sanity, blabbering on about weather conditions before I have explained the true nature of the case."

"It sounds most intriguing."

"To a meteorologist, perhaps. But to the commonplace observer, this is a case of a mysterious disappearance. It is no use, Watson. In order to give you a picture of it I must lower myself to the level of the tabloid journalist and tell the story as if it were a sensational affair. It seems you have at long last won our old argument on how best to narrate the reports of my cases. Anyway, I trust you are familiar with the phenomenon of pilot cutters that are used in harbours to take maritime pilots out to incoming larger vessels."

"Indeed. I have a cousin who is a maritime pilot in Cardiff."

"Splendid. Then you know that the cutters that take the pilots out to the large vessels are rather small affairs, driven by sails or oars."

"I have been taken out on one myself."

"Not a week ago, I was visited by a man who appeared most agitated and flustered. As he entered, he complained of headaches, and it was only after some minutes of relaxing in that sofa, that he introduced himself as a Mr Jack Frome, harbour master of Lydmouth harbour on the south coast west of Brighton. He began by painting a picture of the locality. It is quite a small harbour, but recently they have seen an upsurge in commercial activity trading on the vicinity to the larger

24

harbours of Brighton and Portsmouth. They receive shipments of tomatoes from Spain and sugar from the West Indies. One of the larger West Indian trading vessels, the *Lizzie May*, has stopped at Lydmouth for minor maintenance work on a number of occasions, and it did so once more on the afternoon of November the 28th. The main pilot cutter of Lydmouth is called *Alicia*, and it went out with pilot Richard Wexton at exactly fifteen minutes past three. It was a clear day, and although the sky was already darkening, the harbour master had full sight of the *Lizzie May* from the windows of his office at the quayside. *Alicia* went out with Wexton and three ship's mates on board, but just as it approached the mouth of the harbour, Frome noticed that a thin mist was forming out at sea between the harbour and the trading vessel. In the following minutes, this mist started to grow thicker and thicker, until there was a small but concentrated patch of mist about two miles across separating the harbour from the vessel. Frome swears that in all his life as a seaman he has never seen mist gather so swiftly. The *Alicia* continued out of the harbour and sailed straight into the mist. It never emerged on the other side.

"When the mist cleared away only minutes after the cutter had gone out of sight, Frome could not see any sign of the *Alicia* between the harbour and the trade ship. He waited for nearly two hours, and then he arranged for the spare cutter to be prepared for the journey out to the *Lizzie May*. When it came out of the harbour, with Frome himself on-board, they saw that the *Alicia* was nowhere to be seen in the surroundings of the *Lizzie May*. Reaching the large ship, Frome and his associates started to question the crew, who swore they had not seen any sign of the cutter, despite keeping acute lookout for it, and keeping full watch over the mist since it formed. Frome knows the men in the crew well, and swears there is not a dishonest soul among them. Consequently, there is no accounting for what befell the cutter *Alicia* after it entered the cloud of mist outside Lydmouth harbour."

"Astonishing!" I exclaimed. "I have never heard anything quite like it. Even in the case of the *Marie Celeste,* the disappearance of the crew took place without witnesses, and the ship was only found after the event. But here we have a disappearance right in front of several observers!"

"Exactly, Watson! That was just the aspect that attracted me to the case. I immediately accompanied Frome back to Lydmouth to examine the scene of the mystery for myself."

"I would have expected nothing less from you. What did you find?"

"Precious little. Two days had gone by since the event, and still nothing had been seen or heard either of the boat or its crew. A meticulous search had been conducted along the coast to the east and west of Lydmouth to try and find any remains of the wreck, and three ships had gone out from Lydmouth harbour to scan the area where the cutter had been lost in search of any traces. But not so much as an oar had been found. Upon my arrival, I was taken out with the spare cutter, a boat of similar manufacture to the *Alicia*, and we circled once more the area of the disappearance. I asked Frome and his men about the men who had been on board it. Richard Wexton, he claimed, was an experienced pilot who had been based at Lydmouth for twenty years. He has a wife and three children, two of which are of mature age and have families of their own. He is described as a pillar of the community, much liked by locals and seafaring visitors alike. The three crew members included Thomas Fulford, a local fisherman and old sailor, just as established in Lydmouth as Wexton, and two men who were brothers by the name of Taylor. These two brothers are apparently newcomers to the area, claiming to be shipbuilders from Southampton. You know how suspicious people in small towns can be of strangers, Watson, and the Taylor brothers were no exception. Frome spoke of them with caution, making sure not to put any unfair blame on them, but conspicuously sparing in his praise of them. They are both quite young men, one of them not yet twenty, and they lodge together at one of the harbour taverns. But before I could consider the role these men could have played in the disappearance, I had to try and explain the disappearance itself.

"I continued by examining the *Lizzie May*, which was now anchored in the harbour. I found nothing out of the ordinary, neither by inspecting the hull nor by going through the interiors. The crew is made up to a large extent of indigenous West Indians who speak little English, and the rest of the crew are strangers to Lydmouth, which makes it unlikely that they would have any interest in making away with a small cutter and its crew. It was easy to dismiss a number of possible scenarios by asking what the motive would have been. The problem was that nobody seemed to have stood to gain from the disappearance of the *Alicia* and its crew. In consequence, I saw myself compelled to turn to forces outside of human agency. The explanation had to be connected to the powers of nature or human error. I considered the conditions of the disappearance, and compiled a list of five possible causes: a fire, a large sea wave, a shoal causing the boat to sink rapidly, an encounter with a whale or some other large creature, or an explosion. The problem was that the course of events had to have taken place within a very limited timeframe of no more than four minutes, from the moment when the patch of mist formed to when it cleared away. In this time, the boat could not possibly have been consumed by a fire – unless the mist was no mist but smoke from a fire on a different boat – but it could have sunk as a result of running aground, being attacked by a large animal, consumed by a wave or exploding. All of these eventualities, however, would have left behind a wreck that would have surfaced at least partly, not to mention dead bodies that would eventually have been swept ashore. None of this has happened. I returned to Baker Street from Lydmouth vexed by the lack of clues in this case, and have spent several days testing a number of hypotheses from the comfort of this sitting room. Today, I thought that I had hit upon something promising. I conjectured that the patch of mist in which the cutter was lost was created by artificial means, and have attempted to find the method used by recreating the process in my laboratory."

"That accounts for the mess on the table. And have you found the method?"

"That is not the problem, Watson. A cloud of smoke or vapour could easily be created by human hands, but the question is how could it be done several yards out into the open sea? In conjunction with my experiments, I have tried, as I mentioned, to acquire a complete picture of the weather conditions at Lydmouth that day using as many newspaper reports as I could find. You see the remains of them scattered around you."

"It is a veritable newspaper graveyard. And what does your complete picture indicate?"

"Nothing conclusive. There were no reports of fog anywhere in the vicinity on that day, but the weather was not clear, and the creation of small areas of mist cannot be excluded."

"Could it not have been a cloud of smoke drifting from a nearby fire or factory?"

"Only to thicken once more on the open seas, where it should have been dispersed by the ocean breeze? A queer cloud of smoke, Watson."

"So what are we to make of it all? That the explanation is a supernatural one?"

"Oh Watson, don't be foolish. There is clearly some vital piece of evidence lacking."

"I do hope you will find it, old chap. We don't want another James Phillimore on our hands. After that ordeal, you had to spend a month at a resting home."

"The case haunts me to this day, Watson. It was a perfect vanishing act. His colleague was standing in the street outside, waiting for Phillimore to fetch his umbrella before accompanying him to their office in the City, and inside the house the maid heard the door open and slam shut just seconds before she looked out into the hallway and found it completely empty."

"I remember. In the room to the right, another maid was cleaning, and in the room to the left, the butler was clearing the breakfast table. They heard the door too, but saw no sign of their master. How many weeks did you devote to the case before giving it up?"

"Ten at least. I was positive that the staff of the household had conspired, but in that case, what would they have done to him, and why were there no signs of struggle?"

"And then there was that report from South America. Peru, was it? That a man of his description had checked into a hotel in his name at exactly the same moment that he disappeared in London. Chilling."

"My dear Watson, that must have been a pure coincidence. But it serves to demonstrate how willing people are to welcome impossible solutions."

"Do you think the cutter *Alicia* has ended up in the same place as James Phillimore?"

"Hum! I shall refrain from indulging you in your attempts to allow for supernatural eventualities."

"It only stands to reason to assume that science has not yet explained everything."

"And among those unexplained things you count magic umbrellas and clouds of mist with the power to dematerialise a ship?"

Holmes pulled up his legs into his armchair and peered dreamily into the fire. I enjoyed my cigar in silence for a few minutes, meanwhile picking up one of the newspapers that Holmes had opened on the item that described the *Alicia* affair. There was a picture of Jack Frome accompanying the article, a gentle-looking face framed by a thick chinstrap beard, and I began to contemplate it, musing on this man and his predicament.

"You say that Mr Frome appeared agitated and uneasy when he came to you?" I asked Holmes.

"Yes, and he complained of headaches. But he dismissed my expressions of sympathy, saying that he had regularly occurring headaches and that they usually went away after a while."

"Was it anything more than headaches?"

"What do you mean?"

"I was only reminded of an article I read a few years back about a French physician who described a condition that I have encountered in some of my own patients. It connects migraine headaches with distorted vision or even a loss of vision in one eye."

"You interest me, Watson. Go on."

"Well, there is no mystery about it. The phenomenon is commonly linked to cerebral disturbances, and a decreased arterial blood flow is the probable cause of these distortions, which the medical men term 'auras'. In some it presents itself like zigzagging lines across the field of vision, in some a blurring of the sight on one eye, and in some rare cases a complete loss of sight on one eye."

Holmes looked at me as if frozen stiff. He did not move a muscle for what must have been twenty seconds. Then I could see his eyes moving about as if he was letting his gaze scan across an invisible book in front of him. Finally he rose from his armchair and walked up to the nearest bookcase, from which he took down a folio-sized binder. He carried it to the table, pushed away some of the chemical instruments and placed it there. Untying the ribbon that held the covers of the binder together, he opened it, and I could see that it contained a large bundle of maps. Sea charts, to be exact. Flipping through them, Holmes was clearly searching for one in particular, and when he found it, he made a loud victorious cry.

"Yes, yes, it all fits together. Splendid, my boy! As I have said on numerous occasions, you are a conductor of light. But this time, Watson, you excel yourself. I must admit that you have cracked it, and I am very much in your debt."

"Cracked it? Surely not. A mere sight loss cannot account for the disappearance of an entire ship and its crew!"

"Not on its own, of course, but taken together with the fact that only Frome was following the cutter with his eyes the whole way, and that the patch of mist in all likelihood was not static, but drifted some yards to the side before it cleared away, it is all perfectly obvious. Here, look at this chart of the waters outside Lydmouth. Do you see? Just southeast of Lydmouth is a small group of islands, barely visible from land but close

31

enough to allow a small boat to sail there in a matter of minutes. Now, the waters around here are treacherous, Frome said so himself, and if the conditions are just right, then it is perfectly possible for the *Alicia* to have sailed into the mist, lost its bearings – a small cutter like that has no need for any advanced navigational instruments – and followed along with the patch of mist to the east. Thus, it would have drifted to the left from Frome's point of view, and if it is as you indicated, that he suffered from a blurred field of vision in advance of the migraine headache that he received the next day when he came to see me, then it is likely that he had no view of it. And once the mist cleared away, the cutter, going in the direction of the mist, would have drifted out past the *Lizzie May*, where the captain was keeping lookout for her towards the harbour. Do you see? The *Alicia* needed only go past the *Lizzie May* to become invisible to all who kept a lookout for her. This she could easily have done in the time before the mist cleared away, and once she was on that side, the journey to those islands is a short one, and quite possibly the only way to go once the treacherous undercurrents have taken the upper hand."

"Do you really think this is possible? The undercurrents would have to be very strong for the cutter to go such a long way."

"An experienced sailor knows better than to try and fight currents. The men in the crew had a good reason for not taking any unnecessary risks."

"What's that?"

"Like most sailors, they did not know how to swim."

Holmes walked over to his desk and started scribbling a note. Just then, Mrs Hudson walked in through the door, bearing the latest morning editions.

"Ah, Mrs Hudson," said Holmes. "I need you to take this over to the telegraph office. It is for a Mr Jack Frome of Lydmouth harbour."

I took the newspapers from the landlady and glanced over the front page of *The Times*.

"Holmes!" I cried. "You are too late!"

He looked up from his note and I showed him the headline that read: "Crew of *Alicia* found on Channel island." He took the newspaper and read it while making strange noises of contentment and delight.

"It is just as we deduced! The cutter, when driven off course by the mist and the current, was forced to steer towards the islands to avoid drifting out into the open sea. The captain of the *Lizzie May* admits that all eyes were directed towards the harbour from whence the cutter was expected to come, and if only someone had glanced in the other direction, they would have seen the boat and there would never have been any mystery. The crew of the *Alicia* is reported to be all right in the circumstances, although were found to be suffering from mild dehydration. Oh, and listen to this, Watson: 'Harbour-master Jack Frome also confesses to having withheld the fact that he occasionally suffers from impaired vision due to chronic migraines, a condition which presented itself on the day of the disappearance, and may have contributed to the official's failure to see the cutter as it drifted along with the mist.' Haha! Watson, I am very much indebted to you. Allow me to buy you dinner tonight. Mrs Hudson, you may forget about that telegram."

"But are you not frustrated by the fact that no one will give you credit for actually solving the case without this information?" I said.

"Not in the least. The satisfaction I get from my work comes from myself and not from the acknowledgment of others. It is enough to know that I did solve it, or indeed that there was a solution to it. I often repel at the word 'mystery' that we use for cases like this. There are no mysteries in this world, my friend, only problems that are not yet solved."

"I must say, however," I remarked, "that the promise of a remarkable explanation when the problem is yet unsolved often surpasses the prosaic nature of the real explanation once it is revealed. Seeing the solution to this mystery, for instance, it is plain and simple. And a bit boring."

"That is why people go to magic shows, Watson. They need the illusion of unexplainable mysteries. But I am no conjuror. I am a mechanic, pure and simple, and I solve problems."

"Then perhaps cases like the Phillimore mystery are rather refreshing from time to time?"

Holmes reclined into his armchair once more. "To a collector of fairy-tales, perhaps."

The Adventure of the Cawing Crow

There are, deep within the accumulation of papers in my possession relating to the many cases of Sherlock Holmes, notes of numerous incidents which, if made public, would damage the reputation of many a distinguished aristocrat. I need only intimate the fracas of late that ensued when it was suggested that I publish the data in the case of the Robertson twins and the duplicate drawing-room, and I have more than once been implored to destroy my records of the Otwell House mystery, but there is one case in this category which I am now at liberty to publicise, as all of the major characters in the drama are beyond the reach of public scandal.

It took place in the year '93 or '94 – memory fails me – and provided Holmes with a challenging diversion from a number of protracted commissions from eminent clients. It was a cold day in early spring, and we had just returned from a long morning walk when Mrs. Hudson informed us that a lady was waiting in our sitting room. Holmes examined the calling card.

"Miss Madeleine Crabb of Pettigrew Lodge, Sussex. Her business must be pressing. There was a railway accident on that line only this morning, which must have lengthened her journey considerably."

He climbed the stairs three steps at a time, and I followed readily. We came upon a thin and frail young woman sitting in one of our chairs. She was dressed in a grey plain dress with no decorations, and her brown hair fell in a single long braid across her back. In her hand, she held a simple straw hat of an unfashionable but dainty sort. To me, she was every inch the archetypal girl from the country.

"Miss Crabb, I hope your wait has been brief," said Holmes, pressing her little hand. Then his face changed, and he looked down upon the hand enveloped by his own palm. "But my dear, you are cold as ice! Please draw nearer to the fire."

"Please, do not concern yourself, Mr Holmes," she said. "I am anaemic and always have been. Several doctors have tried to cure my lack of circulation over the years, without succeeding. But I assure you, I am quite all right."

"Nevertheless," Holmes insisted. "The fire cannot hurt. This is my friend and associate Dr Watson, before whom you may speak as freely as before myself."

"That is most comforting," said the lady as we sat down together by the hearth, "for what I have to tell you is most pressing and yet very delicate. It concerns my poor father, who was once a distinguished peer, but is now retired, even though his name is still known in some circles. It is therefore of the utmost importance that what I have to say will not go further than this room."

"You have my assurance," said Holmes.

"And my word as a soldier and servant of Her Majesty," I added. Holmes shot me an amused glance.

"I thank you, gentlemen," the woman replied. "The facts, briefly, are these. My father, Wilfred Crabb, used to be a sharp and opinionated politician who moved in the highest of circles and spent most of his time in London. When he retired, he moved permanently to his newly purchased house at Pettigrew so as to make a clean break with the city life he so loved but was no longer able to lead. The adjustment to this new way of life was trying, but in time, it seemed that he would be able to make the transition, and his urban restlessness gradually gave way to an ability to take pleasure in the attractive scenery of his estate. He started to interest himself in the ancient history of the region, befriended the local vicar who is an amateur archaeologist, and took up the habit of making long walks across the fields and woodland. I quietly started to entertain the notion that my father had found happiness at Pettigrew, until he started to behave strangely. Mr Holmes, perhaps I would do better to consult a medical expert, for my father's problems are basically connected to his health. His mental health."

"You have not wasted your time," said Holmes. "Dr Watson here is a medical man as good as any."

"That is most gratifying, as there are both medical and criminal aspects to my story. My father has gone mad, completely and utterly mad, and there is no way of reasoning with him. His monomania is connected to his archaeological pursuits, but his interest in the local prehistoric remains and Druid monuments has developed from a scholarly fascination to a religious fanaticism. He now proclaims complete faith in pagan gods, and disappears from the house every night to perform strange rituals on the moor that borders onto his land. The local farmers have approached the members of our household, claiming that they have had hens and cats stolen from their homes in the night. Mr Holmes, I believe my father takes these animals and sacrifices them on an old altar stone on the moor that some say used to be part of a Druid shrine."

"What does the vicar say?" I asked.

"I visited him last week in connection with my worries. He admits to having introduced my father into the archaeological remains of the local area, but denies any involvement in fuelling my father's fanaticism, and I believe him. He is a sober and rational man who is much liked in the parish."

Holmes nodded, then leaned forward, pressing his outstretched forefingers together in a gesture of deep concentration.

"Now, Miss Crabb, I would like you to tell us exactly how your father's madness started and how it has evolved."

"Very good. It started quite suddenly one morning, but only after a few days had it taken the form that it has had now for the past few weeks. Ever since we moved to Pettigrew Lodge, it has been the habit of my father and me to take a long morning walk across the meadows that surround our estate. On the morning in question, we chose a path across the moorlands. The weather was fine, and we amused ourselves by noting various species of birds that are indigenous to those parts of the country. In the middle of this moor there are some of the prehistoric remains that had caught my father's interest, including a couple of standing stones and a mound that evidently marks the spot of an old pagan chief's grave. Father spoke to me at length about these things, and his enthusiasm for the subject was at that time so remarkable and rational that he managed to arouse my own curiosity. We had come to a point where the moor is bordered on one side by a copse of trees and an old dilapidated fence that marks the end of our estate. This fence is interrupted at one point by a dead tree trunk that has been incorporated into it as a fence pole. It was there that my father was attracted to the trees by the sound of a bird. To me, it sounded like the cawing of an ordinary carrion crow, but for some reason it made my father stray from the path and walk up to the fence a few yards to our right.

"I stayed on the path and waited for him while he peered in among the trees. He stood there by the fence for a few seconds, and then he turned back. However, as he approached me, I could see a change in his face. The glee and contentment that had infused it earlier were gone, and he looked rather annoyed. I thought that maybe I had made something to offend him, for as he joined me on the path he simply gestured to me to say that we should continue walking. We did so, but it was as if my father was a different man from when we were talking about birds and archaeology only five minutes earlier. He did not speak a word during the rest of the walk, and when I tried to ask him about it, he only turned his head from me. When we returned to the house, he hurried up to his study and locked the door behind him. I did not see him for the next four days. He only ventured from his study at night, long after I had gone to sleep, and went into his bedroom. But according to Mrs. Kilroy, our housekeeper, he slept on top of the bed covers with his clothes on, and he did not change his clothes for at least a week. I believe it was also during these first nights that he began his nocturnal activities."

"How did you become aware of what these activities entailed?" asked Holmes.

"It was our gardener, Mr Brookshaw, who first witnessed it. He had had a particularly long working day, and was in the business of stowing away his gardening tools in the shed, when he suddenly saw something move in the bushes nearby. He called out. There was no answer, but he saw Father running away from there, and he followed him. Father hurried through the garden, down the path that leads to the moor, and Mr Brookshaw ran after him into the woods that lie between our garden and the moor, but there he lost track of him. During the following nights, several members of the household staff came to me to tell me they had seen Mr Crabb going out late at night. It was not until the following week that reports of animal thefts started to come in. By then, I realised I had to take measure, and confronted Father, who had been actively avoiding me ever since that day when he shut himself in his study. He still spent the days there, but we had now established a routine of Mrs. Kilroy going up and giving him his meals on a tray that she left outside the door. One day, I insisted on doing this, and hid myself until the moment when Father opened the door to take in the tray. Then I bolted towards him, forced open the door that he tried to close in my face, and managed to make my way in.

"'Father,' I said, 'I must speak with you.'

"'What is the matter, my child?' he said, quite soberly.

"'I demand to know what is going on!'

"He looked at me, the picture of amused incomprehension. I persisted.

"'What are you doing at night?'

"As we kept staring at each other, the faint smile on his lips started to fade. His look was that of a sane man trapped inside an insane mind. There was a hint of a sad plea, a desperate wish to break free from the madness and join me in the rational world, but hindered by something that would not allow him. He pondered for a moment, then it was as if this restraining madness got the better of him, and the imploring look faded away.

"'My dear child,' he said. 'We must pay tribute to Toutatis, protector of our tribe. He demands a sacrifice, otherwise he will avenge us!'

"And with those words he shut the door before me. I was stunned and puzzled, and walked away from there much saddened. It was now clear to me that Father had taken leave of his senses and had thrown himself into the pagan beliefs that had previously been nothing but a pastime."

Miss Crabb's voice broke, and she lowered her gaze. I ventured to put a hand on her shoulder, but Holmes was completely still.

"How long ago was this?" he asked.

"A week and two days," replied Miss Crabb with some effort.

"And you have not spoken to each other since?"

"Not a word. He avoids me, if he is at all aware of my presence."

"And the nocturnal excursions?"

"Continued uninterrupted until two days ago. Since then I believe he has not left his bedroom. Yesterday I took a walk in the direction that Brookshaw claimed Father had run off to. I came into the woods, and immediately I felt ill at ease, as if the trees brimmed with apprehension. I walked on, however, thinking that I might find something out there that would explain Father's strange behaviour. Only a couple of minutes later, I was met with a horrible sight. Right in front of me on the path, something was hanging from the branch of an old oak tree. I moved closer, and saw to my astonishment that it was a dead black cat, strung up by its neck! I let out a cry and ran to one side, in an effort to move as far away from it as possible. This only brought me face to face with a dead rooster, hanging from its feet from another branch at eye level. The terror of the moment made me disoriented, and I ran around for some moments in this part of the woods, until I encountered another dead cat and the disembodied head of a piglet, strung up in the same way as the other animals. Eventually, I managed to find my bearings, and ran in the direction I had come, returning to the edge of our garden within a few minutes. I met Brookshaw by the rose bushes, and asked him if he had seen the things in the woods, but he knew nothing about it. Concluding that it was in some way connected to Father and his recent mysterious doings, I ran back to the house and started banging on his door, but there was no answer. Panicstricken and seeing no way out, I eventually came to think of you, Mr Holmes. You see, the stories of your exploits were some of Father's favourite reading matter, and since I doubt that the police or a medical doctor would be able to bring any light to this until I have a better understanding of just what is going on, I decided that you were the man to consult."

Holmes let his forefinger run along his lower lip in an expression of deep meditation upon Miss Crabb's story.

"As I said," he remarked, "we have a medical man among us. What would his professional opinion be, I wonder?"

Holmes' and Miss Crabb's eyes were directed at me.

"I agree with Miss Crabb that there are many obscurities in this that need to be sorted out before we can consider Mr Crabb's mental illness," I said. "At this moment, we know virtually nothing about the pathology itself. He has become reclusive, antisocial and seemingly uncaring for his own daughter. But I would say that the most interesting aspect is the suddenness with which these symptoms have appeared."

"Exactly!" replied Holmes. "We must look to the situation and the context before we consider the symptoms." He sprang from his chair and stood by the fireplace, grasping one of his chalk pipes from the mantelpiece without looking at it. I could see that fire in his eyes that showed itself once an intriguing puzzle had nestled its way into his mind. "Now, the careful consideration of human behaviour shows us repeatedly that nothing in it happens suddenly or without reason. I ask you therefore, Miss Crabb, whether you could tell us more about your father's past and about his break with his political entanglements?"

"I could tell you many stories," said our visitor, "about Father's meetings with renowned parliamentarians, not to mention royalty from near and far. Politics was always a passion for him, and he was very much at home in those circles. His debating skills were a source of envy both in his own and in rival parties, but he never seemed to make any real enemies. His main principle was to adhere to the gentlemanly ideal, to retain a courteous and civil tone whenever he voiced his opinions or criticised his colleagues. He was instrumental in introducing a way of speaking in the House of Commons that was modelled on old rhetorical gestures from ancient Rome."

Holmes lit his pipe. "Yes, yes, that is all very good and, I have no doubt, interesting to the man who will eventually compile your father's biography. But surely your father was more than a politician, defining though his politician identity may have been?"

"Father went into politics at a very early age, and he showed an interest already at university, but he worked his way up. He comes from a not very wealthy family in Liverpool, and his father was a shipbuilder. He has told me very little about his early years, and I think his parents died when he was quite young."

"How did he manage to get to university?" I asked.

"There was a schoolmaster at his school in Liverpool who noticed that he had a special talent, and put him up for a scholarship to Cambridge."

I could not help but raise my eyebrows. "Cambridge, eh? Quite the rags to riches story."

"Do you know what school he went to?" asked Holmes.

"I'm afraid not," said Miss Crabb.

"The name of his supportive schoolmaster, perhaps?"

She shook her head. Holmes drew in the smoke from his pipe while eyeing our visitor for a few drawn-out seconds.

"Miss Crabb," he then said. "How many times, exactly, have you actually seen your father since his madness first presented itself?"

The woman appeared to sense unpleasant suspicions behind Holmes' question and looked worried, but she answered in a calm voice.

"The last time I spoke to him was that time a week and two days ago when he was raving about pagan gods. Since then I have only seen him standing at his bedroom window while I was in the garden. Some of the servants have seen him, however. Mrs. Kilroy sometimes lurks by his door when she has brought his tray up to him to make sure he collects it, and she has seen his hands reach out for it on several occasions."

Holmes put down his pipe on the mantelpiece.

"Thank you, Miss Crabb. Your narrative is most intriguing. I advise you to return to Sussex by the first train, and then Watson and I will follow on a train later this afternoon, if that is all right with you? I trust you have no objection to an outing, Watson? Excellent! I hope you will forgive my eagerness, Miss Crabb, but what you have told me contains many worrying details that I would like to give my undivided attention as soon as possible. I ask you not to fear, for all of this may just as well prove to be nothing, but the fact that your father's nocturnal wanderings have ceased to me indicates an ominous development in the course of events. I therefore beg you not to jump to any conclusions until we have all the facts before us."

"I am grateful for your concern, Mr Holmes, and am happy to think that I will see you in Sussex later today."

I admired the young woman's resources for composure, and was surprised to find a stronger woman behind that pale exterior than I had expected. Holmes took her hand graciously and we bid her *au revoir*. It had not been two days since our last excursion into the country, when we brought the affair of the Hargreaves heritage to a close, and I had not had time to unpack my overnight bag from that journey, so I quickly went up to my bedroom to fetch it. When I came back down to our sitting room, Holmes was busy going through his scrapbooks. His packed bag was already lying in the armchair beside him.

"I fear that our young visitor has lived rather a sheltered life. Her father seems not to have told her much about his work, other than that he was successful. We must go to other sources for a more rounded picture of our man! Now, let's see... Crabb, Crabb – ah! Here we are: The right honourable Wilfred Crabb, liberal. Yes, quite a distinguished career. Became an MP in '57, joined the Cabinet as Deputy Minister of Transport, then he appears to have had a series of more or less unofficial advisory positions within the core of the government. His trail grows more obscure the higher he rises in the ranks – a typical course of events in high politics. But my dear brother must know more about him than these meager reports culled from the daily newspapers. I shall call on him at once! An unannounced visit is probably the thing he hates most in this world, but it does him good to have his all too steady foundations unsettled now and again. Watson! Meet me on the platform at London Bridge Station at two o'clock, and we will go together to see our retired politician."

He had spoken without interruption, as was his habit when he did not want me to give my opinion and force him to alter his plans. As he spoke, he grabbed his hat and cane and was out of the door before I had been given an opportunity to confirm our meeting.

It was not until we were reunited in the railway compartment that afternoon that I was able to voice my reactions to Miss Crabb's story.

"I see very little reason," I said as we were rattling out of the southern suburbs, "in connecting Mr Crabb's reclusive behaviour to the grotesque animal executions. That he has been

45

going out in the night at the same time as animals have disappeared is no evidence for suspecting him."

"That is true, Watson, but who else would it be?"

"I think it all points to the gardener. He is the one who claims to have seen Mr Crabb in the night."

"Yes, but why would he go about killing animals?"

"Perhaps they have been intruding in the garden, eating his rosebushes or making trouble?"

"Cats don't eat roses, Watson. Pigs and hens may make a bit of a mess in a well-kept garden, I suppose, but we are not going all the way to Sussex to solve the murders of small animals."

"Then why are we going? I must confess, I cannot quite see what the essence of this mystery is."

Holmes crossed his arms and looked out of the window.

"The essence of the mystery is its disparate curiosities. A grown man with an eminent public record suddenly starts raving about pagan deities. He avoids his beloved daughter seemingly without reason. He makes nocturnal excursions into the nearby woods. The woods are littered with the corpses of animals. All very strange things that we must tie together."

"I don't see how we can. There must be a missing link in this chain."

"Precisely, Watson! We are missing vital parts of the drama. And my experience tells me that such parts are best searched for in the past."

"But there is nothing untoward in the man's past."

"Not that we know of, but his past has its blank spaces."

"Ah! You have gathered information from your brother?"

"I have indeed."

"Was he pleased to see you?"

"I had to ask the page boy at the Diogenes to go and ask him three times before he agreed to see me, and then he kept me waiting in the corridor outside his room for twenty minutes while he finished reading a chapter in his book."

"The epitome of graciousness as always. Did he give you anything useful?"

"Mycroft was exceedingly informative, but his intelligence serves to focus the blank spaces rather than fill them in. Wilfred Crabb is an infamous man in government circles, and he appears to have been an ingenious political strategist working behind the scenes more than a charismatic public figure. His unofficial role in the Cabinet is the most interesting part of his career, and rumour has it he was at one time one of Gladstone's closest advisers, but this work does not seem to have brought Crabb into the fighting ground of politics, as it were. With men like this, however, who work in obscurity and gain a shadowy public image, there is a lot of talk, and Mycroft was at one point assigned to do some research into Crabb's background in order to make sure that there was nothing inappropriate in his past and to put a stop to some of the rumours. He found that what Miss Crabb told us is largely true. He came from a shipbuilding family in Liverpool and came to Cambridge on a scholarship, and there his promising political career began. Only one thing mystified Mycroft, and this was also the very subject of the malicious rumours, namely the scholarship that allowed him to go to Cambridge. The rumours claimed that it had not actually been a scholarship but that he had been sponsored by some or other illustrious person in exchange for certain indecent favours. Mycroft had never been able to ascertain whether this was true, but he found that all records on the scholarship and on how Crabb had funded his time in Cambridge had been lost or deliberately erased."

Holmes paused and allowed the information to sink in.

"My word!" I exclaimed. "But do you think this has bearing on the recent events? I mean, maybe he fiddled his way into Cambridge, but that was half a century ago."

"Yes, it does seem a bit farfetched, does it not? But then again, our past has a strange habit of haunting us just when we think we are far enough from it."

Our speculations had not, as far as I could ascertain, brought us closer to any revelations when we arrived at Crowborough station, where we were met by Miss Crabb and a stable-lad with a pony and trap. We rode east, into an area of wooded hills where the villages were few and far between. After about fifteen minutes, we came down the slope of a pleasant shallow dale and Pettigrew Lodge soon appeared on our right side, a simple three-storey house of rough rubble walls and intricately arranged gables that looked like a well-restored Elizabethan manor house, but upon closer inspection proved to be a newly built Neo-Gothic villa.

"Well, Mr Holmes," said our hostess as we descended from the trap, "I assume you want to try and talk to my father?"

"Certainly not," replied Holmes. "Whatever for?"

Miss Crabb shot me a puzzled glance, and I responded with a shrug of the shoulders.

"But I…" she began.

"Why would he speak to me if he will not even speak to his own daughter? No, that would only be a waste of time. I suggest instead that we take a walk around the grounds of the house and acquaint ourselves with the premises. Perhaps you will be so good as to show us the place where you walked with your father on that fateful evening?"

"Of course, whatever you wish, Mr Holmes."

She walked ahead of us and led us into the garden. Making our way along the flowerbeds, we saw a man of about sixty who was standing in one of them, enveloped by a thick bush, carefully pruning the branches with a short-bladed knife.

"Mr Brookshaw, I presume?" said Holmes, tipping his hat.

"Afternoon, gentlemen. Miss Crabb," said the old man. "You the detective fellow?" he said to Holmes.

"I believe I am. It's quite a garden you have here, Mr Brookshaw. You must be proud of it."

"There's hard work behind it. Every square-inch has been crafted to perfection."

"Impressive, I must say. Are you the sole engineer of it?"

"I am. Well, Mr Crabb used to like to contribute with one or two ideas, but not now that he's gone funny."

"I understand you have seen him going out at night?"

"I have. Several times. Went through the garden and into the woods over there."

"And do you have a theory as to why he did this?"

Brookshaw looked at us with black eyes.

"Paganism," he said, as if it was the most natural thing in the world. "Believe you me, it still has a hold in these parts of the world. The simple folk are still very superstitious. Once in a while it gets into the head of a gentleman who is bored with life and needs something exciting to hold onto. Mr Crabb was just such a man. Now that politics was no longer a part of his life, he needed something to replace it."

"So he replaced politics with paganism?" I said.

"That's right."

"Doesn't really sound like a natural transition."

"You underestimate the power of paganism, sir."

"Either that or he overestimates the power of politics," said Holmes with a smile. "Would you object to our having a little look in your toolshed, where I understand you saw Mr Crabb one night?"

Brookshaw looked Holmes up and down. "I did not actually see him in the shed, only outside, but you are perfectly welcome to look at it. It is there, by the holly. The door's open."

"Thank you very much for your help, Mr Brookshaw." Holmes promenaded up to the little shed while I stayed with Miss Crabb, who started to talk to her gardener about their current trouble with moles. When Holmes returned he was smiling, but he said nothing and only led the way onwards. I was curious as to why he had conversed so briefly with the gardener. To me, he was a suspicious character whose involvement in this affair I presumed to be more insidious than it appeared, and so I queried him about it once we were out of earshot.

"My dear friend, we have no more reason to suspect Mr Brookshaw than we have to suspect any inhabitant of the area. Mr Crabb's strange behaviour began when he and Miss Crabb were far away from Brookshaw's domain. If in some way he played a part in that moment, stalking them on their way or some such thing, then what did he do, and why has he done nothing for several weeks? If he had sinister motives, his actions should have left some sort of traces."

"I agree with you, Mr Holmes," said Miss Crabb. "Brookshaw has been with us for a long time and he has always been most loyal, thinking very highly of my father."

"But still," I said, "a major part of this is based on Brookshaw's testimony. What if he is lying about seeing Mr Crabb at night? Then there is nothing to connect him with the dead animals."

"Then who strung them up?" said Miss Crabb.

"Well, I don't know. I'm just saying that we cannot assume anything."

Holmes made a sweeping gesture with his forefinger. "My dear Watson, I am assuming nothing at all. I am quite certain that if Brookshaw had done anything suspicious he would not wait around for us to arrive. Now, of course it is quite possible that Brookshaw strung up the animals, but we must acquire an overall picture before delving deeper. This is the way into the woods, I take it?"

"It is, Mr Holmes," replied our host, "but is it really necessary to go in there? I would not like to see those animals again."

"I am afraid it will be absolutely necessary, Miss Crabb. But if you feel uneasy please stay by Watson's side. He is well versed in the noble art of escorting."

He winked at me and walked a few steps ahead of us until we encountered the first of the slaughtered beasts. We had been walking down a narrow path that led straight into a thick grove of trees. Right in front of us, a black cat, showing some signs of decay, was hanging from a piece of household string that was attached to a tree branch some three yards above our heads. Holmes moved close to it – a bit closer than I thought appropriate – and studied the animal and the rope.

"Interesting, very interesting. The cat appears to have been rather clumsily hacked to death with something similar to a kitchen knife. It is hardly the skilled work of a poacher."

Miss Crabb winced at hearing his description.

"Holmes, please," I begged. "Must you be so pathological?"

He did not appear to take any notice of me. "Hm... But the most striking thing is undoubtedly the knot. This has not been tied by an ordinary gardener. There is quite a different type of expertise in evidence here."

I tried to get a close look at the knot while keeping a somewhat healthier distance than Holmes. It did not look very extraordinary to me. It was not a hangman's noose, that I could see, but other than that it efficiently kept the animal elevated from the ground I could conclude very little about it. The mere sight of it made me uneasy, and I hoped that Holmes' examination of it would prove brief.

"I don't think there is any need for us to examine the other animals," said he to my great relief, then adding: "Let us continue into the woods."

"Holmes," I said. "Miss Crabb is starting to look pale."

"Pale?" He said it as if it was a new word to him. "With all this fresh air and exercise? There is really nothing to be afraid of here."

"Apart from a series of ritually slaughtered animals," I added.

"Oh, hardly ritually. I think that the only purpose for these hanging animals is one that they have already served."

"And what is that?" asked Miss Crabb with a curiosity that seemed to outrival her anxiety.

"To deter the people of Pettigrew Lodge from wanting to go through the woods."

"Do you really think so?" I said. "It is not some form of perverse pagan ritual?"

"Watson, why would a lonely old man entertain himself by killing small animals in the middle of the night if there was no underlying motive to it?"

"You may be right. But why should people be hindered from going through the woods?"

"We shall have to see, won't we?"

52

Holmes led the way through the trees, and we passed a number of hanging animals that I took care to lead Miss Crabb past so that she would not have to lay her eyes on them again. In due time, the trees came to a halt, and a primitive old stone wall marked the border to the adjacent field that stretched out a good two miles ahead of us.

"Miss Crabb," said Holmes, "you mentioned a point in the fence at the other end of the moor where there was a dead tree trunk. Do you think you can find it for us?"

"I am certain of it," she replied. "I know this moor like the back of my hand."

She strode fearlessly ahead, climbing over the wall without effort and starting the long trek across the moor without even looking back to see if we were keeping up. White clouds had been looming over the sky for the better part of the day, but now they were slowly dispersing, and as we came out of the shade the sunlight was rather hot on our necks. I felt obliged to remove the Norfolk jacket I habitually wore on excursions like this, realising that we were closer to summer than I had acknowledged. Holmes walked in silence, with a sense of purpose that he reserved for the most pivotal moments of his investigations, and I knew from experience that most of the links in the chain were in his head already, and that he only needed one or two to confirm his suspicions. What those suspicions were, however, I could not say. My own suspicions were as yet unspecified. But, like Holmes, I had the notion that what was missing in our picture of the scenario was possibly another player, someone from the outside.

We had almost arrived at the place where the moor ended, and the wooden fence marking the end of the estate extended along another forest, when Holmes suddenly stopped and looked about himself.

"Do you see the mounds, Watson?" he said and pointed, first in one direction, then in another. "Ancient prehistorical burial mounds from the time before Britain had been christianised. The Crabbs are not the first people to take up residence in this area."

"Wilfred Crabb recognised that," I said. "The question is if the history of this place has anything to do with our case?"

"I have not ruled out that possibility."

I looked out on the barren moor.

"I cannot see that there is anything here that the dead animals were meant to warn us about."

Miss Crabb, who was a few yards ahead of us, called out and pointed at a large dead tree standing as a guard to the entrance of the forest.

"Capital!" Holmes exclaimed. "Now, remind us, Miss Crabb. What happened?"

"We were walking along this narrow little path that has been tramped up in the grass here, and it was about here that father stopped and looked into the woods."

"And then he was attracted to the fringe of the woods?" I said.

"By the sound of a bird," Holmes added. "A cawing crow."

"Whoever would react to such a common sound? Especially here in the midst of the countryside."

"Only a madman, surely." Holmes peered into the darkness of the trees with a dreaming gaze for a few moments, then he turned to Miss Crabb. "What lies beyond the forest?"

"Bridle," she said. "A very small village consisting of a small cluster of houses and a church."

"Is that where the local vicar resides?"

"Yes."

"Then we must pay him a visit."

Holmes appeared most adamant in exploring every inch of the area, and although Miss Crabb and I were both tired and hungry, we indulged him, and so Miss Crabb led the way through the forest to the village of Bridle. I counted not more than five or six houses scattered around a village green. One of them was the vicarage, but we were spared the effort of knocking on its door, for just as we stepped onto the green, we were stopped by a man calling out to us and approaching. He introduced himself as Martin Flint, the vicar of Bridle. He seemed quite impressed by my friend's presence in his little village, but was more focused on Miss Crabb, at whom he directed a few comforting words.

"Mr Flint," said Holmes, "did you see any preliminary signs of the lunacy that has inflicted Mr Crabb?"

"None at all," said the vicar. "I spoke to him only a couple of days before his isolation, and then he was as normal and as sharp as ever."

"You conversed on your common passion, I take it?"

"As a matter of fact, we did. He was taking an increasing interest in the prehistorical remains of the area."

"Was he planning any excavation work?"

Flint looked a bit startled by this question.

"I don't think so. Mr Crabb's interest was on a strictly literary basis."

"I see. But you are yourself an amateur archaeologist, I understand? That dirt underneath the fingernails can be so hard to get rid of, can it not?"

Flint looked down on his hands and evidently realised that several of his fingernails had dirt under them.

"Oh yes. Well, I am quite enthusiastic about it. I have been conducting a survey of the moor, excavating some of the barrows there a few weeks ago, and right now I am doing some digging close to the church, where I have reason to believe there has once been a pagan temple."

"How fascinating! Did you excavate all the barrows?"

"No, there are several of them. I only dug out two or three, but I found nothing spectacular. Mr Crabb was with me on one occasion, and we exchanged some interesting speculations upon the age and structure of these burial mounds."

Holmes nodded and looked at the little cottages that surrounded us.

"Who lives in the village?"

Flint once again looked a bit vexed by this curious man's random series of questions. "Old folks, mainly. This community is slowly fading away."

"And I presume the cottages have been in the same families for generations?"

"Precisely. Apart from the old smithy, of course, which was empty until a few months ago."

"A newcomer?" I asked.

"An old man. Seemed like he wanted to come here for some peace and quiet. He was seen to arrive one day with a large trunk and then he settled into the little house. I went over there a few times to welcome him to the village, but he never opened the door even though I could see he was lurking inside. He seemed harmless nonetheless."

"He never goes out?"

"Not that I have seen. Only I think he has left, for the place is starting to show signs of being deserted again."

Mr Flint indicated a small dilapidated cottage that lay just where the village bordered onto the woods. Holmes gestured at us to stay where we were, and then he quickly went up to the house, walking stealthily up to the window to peer in. There he stood for a minute or two before rejoining us again.

"The place is empty. There is nothing more for us to do here. Let us return to the house."

We bid farewell to the gracious vicar, and started on our way back through the forest. As we were nearing the moor, Miss Crabb suddenly stopped on the path and turned to us.

"Did you hear that?"

"What was it?" said Holmes.

Miss Crabb started to smile to herself.

"I'm sorry, I am jumping at shadows. It was only a crow."

"It is understandable that you should react to their sound," I remarked.

"Yes, I suppose so. There it is again."

"Indeed," said Holmes.

We walked on. As I looked back, I saw that Holmes was standing still, looking up into the tree tops.

"Holmes, what's up?"

"What indeed, Watson," he said furtively. "What indeed."

It was impossible to get Holmes to sit down to dinner when we returned to Pettigrew Lodge. He was giddy and restless, and although Miss Crabb promised that she would try to let her father accept him after dinner, both she and I could not hide that we were very hungry after the afternoon's work. Holmes insisted that we ate while he lingered in the billiard room smoking a few cigarrettes. I tried to keep up a decent conversation with Miss Crabb on commonplace matters as we dined on our own, but although she seemed to appreciate my effort and tried to chat politely with me, it was apparent that she was nervous, and, I suspect, started to doubt that my friend's presence would alter her unfortunate predicament. It was with relief, therefore, that I saw how the door into the billiard room flung open once we were finished with our dessert, and Holmes came rushing in, looking as if something both troubling and delightful was on his mind.

"Miss Crabb," he said. "I must see your father immediately!"

"Mr Holmes," she replied, "why the sudden hurry?"

"Because this is a most grave matter, Miss Crabb, and it must come out in the open once and for all."

Miss Crabb rose from her chair. "Mr Holmes, will you tell me what you have discovered?"

Holmes looked at her, then at me, calming down slightly, as if my presence reminded him of his manners. "Will you both please come with me into the billiard room?"

He led us into the adjoining room, and walked across the floor to a small nook in the wall next to the opposite door.

"Do you know what this picture represents?"

He was pointing at a medium-sized oil painting of a ship, rather crudely executed in a manner that I had seen a hundred times, and which is quite common for marine paintings. It was placed in a dark corner nestled in between a bookcase and a door frame, and it was unassuming to say the least.

Miss Crabb studied it closely. "No, Mr Holmes, I cannot say that I do. This house is full of paintings, some of which come from my father's collections and some of which came with the house when we purchased it."

"I see. And your father has never spoken of it?"

"No. I don't see why he should. He is not a sailor. As far as I know, he has hardly been on a boat."

Holmes chuckled and looked at the picture. "I am afraid you have been slightly misled in that aspect, Miss Crabb. For you are looking at the vessel on which your father served as shipmate."

The young woman frowned and took two or three steps back.

"Mr Holmes, what are you saying?" she said despairingly. "This is simply not true."

"I'm afraid it is. You see, there never was a scholarship that funded your father's university education. He went through it on his own endowment."

"I am sure I have no idea what you are talking about."

"Perhaps it would be better to sit down. Let us move over to these little easychairs. There. Are you comfortable, Miss Crabb?"

"Please don't fret, Mr Holmes. Will you explain yourself?"

"I will. The name of the ship in the picture is the *SS Cordelia*. It is rather a famous ship, actually, which is why even I, who am not really much informed in nautical matters, have heard of it. I am an expert in crime, Miss Crabb, and I know of that ship because it was connected to a crime some years ago. It was before any of us were born, actually, but the story of it still lingers as one of the most ingenious swindles in recent history, and I remember making a close study of it in younger days when I was something of an amateur student of criminology. It was a merchant ship sailing in 1829 for Caracas, on a cargo of coal, and returning back to England with a cargo of rubber. The captain was a man named Morris Addleton, a promising young mariner who had already been on several trips to the Caribbean. He was a well-liked and skilled seaman with an experienced crew, which is all the more remarkable considering the outcome of the journey. For on its way back, the *Cordelia* went missing, and about a month after its expected return to England, it sailed into Liverpool Docks with only a third of its original crew remaining and one of the mates acting as a substitute captain.

"It was said that the *Cordelia* had sailed into a violent storm somewhere in the Antilles, in which it had almost capsised, and that this was where the crew had suffered its catastrophic loss. An investigation showed, however, that there were no reports of storms from other ships who had sailed in that area at the same time, and that only a week after the ship had left Caracas, one of its lifeboats had gone ashore on the island of Martinique, bearing a small portion of the ship's crew, including Captain Addleton. Addleton had claimed that some insurgent men of the otherwise loyal crew had stirred up into mutiny, which had evolved into a fight between the mutineers and those that remained supportive of the captain. In the end, Addleton and his followers had been forced to abandon the ship. This whole story was much reported in the newspapers of the time, and everyone expected a great and dramatic trial to follow, but for some reason Captain Addleton never returned to England to testify, and there was never a substantial enough case to hold the returning sailors, and so the whole thing just faded away.

"Since then, however, new information has come to light. One of the sailors who returned with the *Cordelia* confessed in his dying days that the reason for the scuffle between the men was that word had been spreading among them that their captain was bringing home with him a treasure chest that he had somehow acquired while the ship was at port. One of the men, a Mr Robert Stroke, had stirred menace by persuading his fellow sailors that they all had equal part in this treasure by making sure it came safely back to England, and the ensuing mutiny was all about this treasure. The treasure did actually exist, as the mutineers found out after Addleton and his men had left the ship. It was a chest full of nuggets of pure gold that Addleton's brother, who was an explorer and anthropologist in South America, had collected on his travels in the Andes, and which he had asked his brother to bring home to their father's estate for safe keeping. But when the ship came to Liverpool, there was no sign of the chest, even though several of the men would later confess to having seen it during the trip, and that they even managed to open it and confirm its alleged contents.

"So what happened to it? It is very simple. In the small hours of the morning before the *Cordelia* was about to sail into Liverpool, Stroke carried the chest up on deck, tied it to a long rope with a float at the other end and threw it over the side. He took a great risk, dumping the loot in such a heavily trafficked sea, but this way only he knew where it was and how to get it. He also managed to make away with the evidence that the motive for the mutiny was anything other than a sense of injustice."

I glanced at Miss Crabb, whose face did not try to hide that she had been quite gripped by Holmes' story.

"What happened to him?" she said.

"He disappeared from view."

"So how do you know about how he hid the chest?"

"Because a long time ago when studying this case, I spoke to the old fisherman who rowed him out to the place to pick it up."

"Remarkable!" I cried.

"But I still don't understand," said Miss Crabb. "If it is a famous ship, then there must be hundreds of pictures of it."

"Not really," said Holmes. "Paintings of that sort are not usually reproduced or copied."

"So you mean to say that my father was on board the *Cordelia*?"

"I mean to say more than that, Miss Crabb. I mean to say that he is Robert Stroke."

"Surely you are taking this a bit too far, Holmes," I protested. "Only because of that painting?"

"No, not only because of that. I instantly recognised that painting because I have seen it before quite recently."

"Where?"

"In the empty house in the village. I looked in through the windows and that painting looked familiar. It was only when I saw it once more here that I recalled the story. And then, of course, there is the evidence of the cawing crow."

"The crow?" said Miss Crabb. "What of it?"

"You see, when you said that your father walked over to that fence at the sound of a cawing crow, it seemed strange to me, and I was certain that something more significant had made him go over there. Then on our walk back from the village we heard it again, only to me, it was not the sound of a common crow. So I looked up into the treetops and saw something truly remarkable."

Holmes paused and studied our faces. Miss Crabb's eyes were fixed on him. I myself was eager to hear the rest of his reasoning.

"What was it, Holmes?"

"It was a parrot."

"A parrot?" said Miss Crabb.

"Quite so. You see, in the newspaper reports on the *Cordelia* affair, Captain Addleton is repeatedly described with one conspicuous attribute – a parrot. When I saw the parrot flying about in the tree tops, I understood that this was a vital clue, but I only appreciated its meaning when I saw the picture here."

"What do you mean, Mr Holmes? This is still not quite clear to me."

Holmes rose.

"Miss Crabb, I think it is high time that I spoke with your father. Will you escort us upstairs?"

Miss Crabb did as he asked, even though she continued mumbling that he was unlikely to see us. As we came to the door, Holmes stopped Miss Crabb's hand in mid-air as it was about to knock.

"Please," he said. "Allow me." And then he turned towards the door, exclaiming: "Robert Stroke, open this door!"

It only took five seconds before there was a rustling sound and the door was opened wide. Behind it stood a man of advanced years, but whose mixture of curiosity and guilt made him look like a young man, nay, a boy. He looked at us as if he recognised in us old acquaintances, but acquaintances that he had no wish to be reunited with.

"Mr Stroke, I perceive?" said Holmes.

"Where have you heard that name?" said the old man.

"It was all over the frontpages a few years ago."

"Many years ago! Nobody remembers."

He was just about to close the door again, when his daughter stepped up and put her hand on it.

"Father? It's me, Madeleine. Will you not explain to me what is happening? I deserve to know the truth."

Crabb hung his head and when he looked up again there were tears in his eyes. "I'm sorry, Madeleine. I am so very sorry."

"But Father, what is the matter?"

"Stay away from me, Madeleine. I am a bad man."

"I don't care what you did when you were young."

"What about what he did two weeks ago?" said Holmes.

Miss Crabb looked at him, then at her father, demanding an explanation with her anxious gaze.

"Two weeks ago," said Holmes, "your father committed murder."

"What?" cried Miss Crabb. "Is this true, Father? What am I saying? Of course it is not true! Mr Holmes, how dare you!"

"Your father cannot deny it. Two weeks ago, you and he were walking when he was drawn to the fringe of the woods by the sound of a bird, a sound that he recognised all too well but had hoped never to hear again. It was the sound of Captain Addleton's parrot. Peering into the woods, Mr Crabb saw him. Addleton had come to Bridle to settle matters once and for all with Robert Stroke, and so he walked daily in the woods, hoping one day to encounter his mortal enemy. And when he did, they agreed to meet in the night and confront each other. I do not know exactly what Addleton had planned for Stroke, but whatever it was, it misfired, and the avenger once more became the victim of the resourceful Stroke, leaving the bird to fend for itself in the woods. What did you use, Stroke? Was it one of Brookshaw's gardening tools?"

"Holmes," I said, "you are forgetting one thing. There is no dead body."

"No, there isn't. Stroke had it all planned, as usual. Only the day before he had assisted the vicar in excavating one of the barrows on the moor. He knew that the earth there was still loose. It would not be too difficult to drag the body there. Perhaps you even agreed to meet there, thus making the whole thing easier for yourself?"

Mr Crabb's eyes had turned black, and he looked upon Holmes with what I feared was murderous intent.

"But why the dead animals?" asked Miss Crabb.

"A most necessary distraction. Firstly, it established once and for all that your father had become mad and was sacrificing animals – a ruse that was essential, both so that he could bury the body at night and avoid the one person before whom it would be difficult to lie. Secondly, the hanging animals deterred the people in the house – you especially, Miss Crabb – from walking through the woods and out on the moor until the traces of the murder were gone. Connecting his madness to his previous interest in the local archaeology was also a way of making it seem credible, you understand. But, ironically, it was the dead animals that put me on the right track to begin with, for they had been tied up with a very special knot known only to sailors."

When Holmes concluded his explanation, there was a second when we all looked at each other in some form of anticipation, as if we were both wondering what would happen and expecting something to happen. Mr Crabb slammed his door shut as he had threatened to do a few minutes before, and Holmes tried to push it open in vain.

"This is ominous to say the least. Miss Crabb, is there any other way into this room?"

"Only through the window, but we are one floor up."

"That would be the western wall. Unless I am mistaken it is covered in ivy?"

"Yes, but it is old and perishing."

"Cannot be helped, there is no time to lose. Watson, come with me!"

And I rushed with Holmes out into the garden, leaving the poor young woman to bang on her father's bolted door. I knew just what Holmes was fearing, and if he was right it was only a matter of minutes before it would be too late to save the old man from death by his own hand. As we reached the western wall, I saw that the ivy did reach up to the first floor, but it was only a leafless skeleton of a trunk and I doubted that it would hold for climbing. Holmes did not hesitate, however, and was halfway up it before I could stop him. He found a foothold on a ledge just by the window in question, which allowed me to climb up after him. It was not such a precipitous effort as I had thought, and as I came to the window I saw the sight that had stopped Holmes from climbing in.

The door that Mr Crabb had bolted was now open again, and father and daughter were standing on the threshold, locked in each other's embrace. Somehow, in the time it had taken Holmes and me to go out of the house and climb the ivy, Miss Crabb had persuaded her father to open the door, and, with the aid of her female powers of conciliation, generated by herself the idyllic family reunion that we were now witnessing.

Holmes would say to me, when we were reminiscing over this case a few days later, that Miss Crabb's pacifying abilities had an equal share to his own logical reasoning in seeing the case to a fulfilling conclusion. Had it not been for Wilfred Crabb's love for his daughter, he might very well have completed his regression to the devious plotting shipmate that his reunion with Morgan Addleton had triggered, but in between his sailor youth and his autumn-years murder, Robert Stroke had become Wilfred Crabb, a decent and good-natured politician and family man, and it was this second nature that made the man confess his deeds and give himself up to the local police. It was never reported in the newspapers at the time, however, that the unexpected return to public life of shipmate Robert Stroke sprung from the retirement of the Right Honourable Wilfred Crabb, and it was for the benefit of his daughter that this connection was never made known. Sadly, however, Crabb only survived a year in the harsh conditions of

Dartmoor prison. His daughter eventually changed her name and emigrated to Canada where I understand she married and now lives in blissful obscurity.

It always seemed to me curious why Wilfred Crabb should go to such extreme and strange lengths to divert the attention from his crime and give him time to bury the remains of Captain Addleton, but although his madness was a deception, the thing it was designed to hide was a madness in itself, of sorts. The ancient barrow on Pettigrew moor was eventually excavated by the police, and Addleton's corpse retrieved so that it could be given a proper burial. To my great surprise, his anthropologist brother was still alive, and attended the funeral along with Madeleine Crabb, who insisted upon compensating him from her own inheritance for the gold that her father had once stolen from him.

One spring evening – I think the year was ninety-six – Holmes made a suggestion I believe he had never done before.

"Do you want to go to the pub, Watson?"

I was a bit taken aback by this query, but since I was well aware that Holmes was the most unpredictable person one could imagine, my surprise was only mild.

"Are you thirsty?" I said. "If it's a drink you want, my club…"

"I have no interest whatsoever in the beverages provided by public houses," he replied.

"What induces your proposal, then?"

"Only this."

He handed me a crumpled piece of paper. It read:

"Please Mr Holmes, if you would pay a visit to Princess Louise in the near future, I promise to provide you with a problem that might satisfy your thirst for the unusual. A. Winstanton."

I looked over the curious message a few times, but it puzzled me and it seemed like the person who had written it was being deliberately obscure.

"Well," I said, "I would venture to say that, since this is obviously a royal commission, the messenger – this Winstanton fellow – has written it in some sort of code, which I am sure is apparent to you, but completely baffles me."

Holmes knitted his brow. "Code, you say? And wherein lies the code?"

"I have no idea. But the message has virtually no information in it, so I fancied the real message was somewhere between the lines. In the amount of words or something of that sort."

"Ha! What an interesting interpretation, Watson. You never cease to astound me."

"Am I anywhere near the truth?" I asked, exposing my lack of belief in my theory.

"Afraid not, old man." Holmes took back the paper. "Your theory of a royal commission is most intriguing, not to say flattering, but if this really was a commission from the actual Princess Louise, then why would the only real piece of information in the message be the stating of her name? No, I am more inclined towards the simple interpretation."

"I thought mine *was* the simple interpretation."

"The interpretation of the name as referring to one of Her Majesty's daughters was the simple part, then it forced you into considering quite unlikely things, including ciphers."

"All right, I got the point the first time."

"No, the name 'Princess Louise' must surely refer to the celebrated public house of that name which opened a few years ago in Holborn. It is not an ordinary pub, in the sense that it caters to a somewhat higher class of people than most London public houses, and as such it is rather lavishly furnished. Mr Winstanton I take to be the proprietor of the establishment, and although his message is vague on the details, the writing does betray some of the pub-owner's habitual taste for banter, what with referring to my 'thirst for the unusual'."

"You don't think it is a trap of some sort?"

"You are right to be suspicious, Watson. It does seem like an attempt to lure me into a trap, but who would trap me in such a public place as that? The purpose of the note is probably just to arouse my curiosity, and in this endeavour, it has succeeded. So, how about it, Watson?"

I was not one to go against Holmes' wishes when he was on the scent, and I was just as intrigued by the prospect of adventure as he was, so I threw away the newspaper I had been reading, and within a quarter of an hour a hansom deposited us at the patriotically named establishment of the message. It was only six o'clock, but already the place was filling up with a colourful collection of assorted clerks from the surrounding office buildings, as well as academics and intellectuals streeming down from nearby Bloomsbury. But this collection did not automatically mean a mixture, for as Holmes had mentioned, this was a more sophisticated pub than the average one, and as we entered through one of its two entrances, a corridor led into four separate rooms, all of them abutting onto the same counter, but divided by high walls decorated with panes of frosted glass. The first room that we looked into was the noisiest, and the men assembled there could be described as skilled workers, or what some have termed the "labour aristocracy". Here, however, they were at the bottom of the pyramid, for the next room contained a more modest group of well-dressed men who looked to me like lowly clerks and the odd office boy, and the ascension continued in the next rooms, until the back room, which was very much like stepping into the lounge of the Athenaeum.

It was here that a man approached us. He seemed a bit out of place among the distinguished gentlemen scattered around the room, as his appearance rather called to mind a dubious businessman or vulgar music-hall proprietor, with flamboyant ginger side-whiskers and a gold-embroidered waistcoat.

"Ah, Mr Holmes," he said in a strong voice which reverberated throughout the room. "My name is Arnold Winstanton, the proprietor of this humble establishment. I'm glad my note managed to lure you here."

"It lured me this far," said Holmes, "but I proceed no further without more information. The note was sparse in the extreme. Why this secrecy?"

"Well, if you will at least proceed up the stairs with me, all will be explained."

Mr Winstanton showed us to a flight of stairs at the back of the lounge, and we climbed up to a private bar which, it seemed for our benefit, had been emptied of people. Winstanton invited us to sit in a couple of comfortable leather armchairs by a roaring fire before taking a seat himself, inspecting us with a pleased, almost jeering, smile. "So, gentlemen, you were wondering why I asked you here."

"Is it anything to do with the thieving barman?" asked Holmes.

"No." His smile vanished in less than a second. "Certainly not. What barman would that be?"

"The one downstairs, big fellow, short black hair and handlebar moustache. He has been stealing from your register for at least a few weeks now."

"Burleigh? What nonsense! What makes you think that?"

"He hides the money in a secret pocket inside his waistcoat which bulges conspicuously. The fabric on the front of the waistocat has become stretched as a result of it."

Winstanton impatiently sidestepped the matter. "No, it is not about that."

"I see," said Holmes. "Then is it perhaps the matter of your deceitful wife?"

"What?" Winstanton's eyes looked as if they were going to fall out of their sockets.

"Very well. Proceed."

Winstanton now looked utterly confused. "Why do you think my wife is deceiving me?"

"It is of no consequence. Please state your case."

The man took a few deep breaths to compose himself. "It is simply because I have the highest respect for your powers of observation that I have asked you to come here, Mr Holmes, and I hope that you may assist me."

"I shall certainly do my best."

"All right, then. Mr Holmes, I believe the Princess Louise is haunted. On four consecutive nights now, customers have complained of being robbed of their possessions, but despite exhaustive efforts to obtain the missing items and to apprehend the pickpockets, there has been no solution to the mystery. After the first two incidents, an Inspector Gregson came to investigate, and he suspected that a gang of pickpockets is operating in the premises. He had four of his men in civilian clothes infiltrating the visitors an entire evening, but nothing came out of it. Not even when a gentleman complained of having lost his pocketbook and Gregson ordered all the customers not to leave. Mr Holmes, each and every one of the customers that night were thoroughly searched, but nothing was found! Despite this, Gregson arrested three men on suspicions grounded upon the fact that the infiltrating policemen had not been able to survey them sufficiently. But all three men had to be released, since all of them proved to be entirely respectable City clerks with not a flaw in their character. And yet it goes on. Last night, three customers had their pockets picked, one of his purse and two of their watches."

"And what of the staff?" inquired Holmes.

"I trust them all, including Burleigh. He has a seedy past, and maybe he takes a few notes from the till now and then, but he nor any of the others could have picked the customers' pockets since they are all behind the counter, and the counter, as you know, is circular and never opens up into the rooms. I employ a young girl who goes around and picks up the empty tankards from the tables, but naturally I have searched her belongings as well as the kitchen and the kitchen staff without success. I can but think that whoever snatches things from our visitors has the ability to become invisible. A ghost!"

Winstanton broke off and produced a handkerchief to wipe his brow. Holmes was silent and did not move a muscle in his face.

"But surely," I said, "it must be very difficult to keep track of everybody who comes and goes. I'm sure the explanation must be that the culprit is extremely skilled at sneaking away inconspicuously and was even able to do so when the police was present."

"Impossible!" cried Winstanton. "The moment that gentleman noticed his pocketbook was gone, the inspector blew his whistle and his men stopped everybody from passing through the doors."

"I see."

Winstanton looked at Holmes. "You are a man of few words," he said.

Holmes looked up from his thoughts. "The problem is interesting, but the solution can only be a simple one. The stolen goods must be hidden somewhere in the premises since they have not been taken from here, at least not when the police was present. The thief is, as you said, Watson, most professional, and the secret to his success must be a very special trick of the trade. Tell me, Mr Winstanton, how would you describe the men that fell victim to the thefts?"

The publican shrugged.

"Quite ordinary, I suppose, like most of our customers. Some I would say belonged to the lower office working class, respectable but hardly men of means. But most of the afflicted men were very distinguished gentlemen indeed. One of them was a Lord, if I'm not mistaken."

"And have the thefts occurred in any special compartment of the pub or in different rooms?"

"There have been incidents in both the front and back rooms."

"And how did the victims call attention to their thefts?"

"By calling out, of course, as is the custom. 'Stop thief.' 'I've been roobed.' Something like that."

"All of them?"

"Yes."

"Yes. It is of course the time lapse between the actual pocketpicking and the discovery of the theft that is critical. Most street pickpockets operate in gangs and the party who actually does the stealing immediately hands over the stolen goods to an accomplice who passes by and then walks off in a completely different direction than the first party. This second man also generally hands the goods over to a third person as a precaution. Thus the man that is most easily apprehended – namely the actual thief – is almost never the man who has the loot, and so there is seldom any evidence against him. But why would a gang of pickpockets choose the interior of a public house instead of the street where it is so much easier to get away? Admittedly it is a public house with a wealthier clientele than most others, but the public street also has a wealthy clientele. No, I think we can exclude the possibility that we are dealing with a gang of pickpockets. The thief works alone."

"I find that quite unlikely," said Winstanton.

"There are other ways of disappearing after the act has been committed." Holmes lowered his gaze. His next words were directed to himself. "Yes. Yes. That must be it." And then he looked up again. "Well, I thank you, Mr Winstanton, for providing us with a most intriguing case. If you don't mind, Dr Watson and I will now go down into the saloon bar and have a couple of beers."

"At my expense of course, Mr Holmes!" said Winstanton. "I trust I will hear from you?"

"Sooner than you might think."

And so we were escorted back downstairs, and Winstanton left us to take care of other business. Holmes, having been slightly pensive while listening to the publican's story, now seemed more cheerful, and he knocked his pot of beer against mine with the fervour of a drunken sailor. "Your very good health, Watson!"

"You sound very optimistic all of a sudden."

"Well, yes and no. I am optimistic concerning this case and its potential of becoming an interesting one, but at the same time, all vital clues point to a very tangled skein indeed, and one that may have dark dimensions."

"How so? You suspect the involvement of some sort of criminal organisation?"

"That is a question of definition. I think we are dealing with a very cunning adversary here, and I suspect that he may not be quite what we expect. But I'm afraid I have no working hypothesis as yet. What about you, Watson? You were pretty silent up there. What theories do you have?"

"Well, if this man really is working alone, as you think, then I would guess that he makes use of disguises rather than accomplices."

"Brilliant, Watson. Why do you think so?"

"A lot of pickpockets do it. Why, almost every week the papers report on the latest deeds of the 'swell mob'. In this case, however, it is a question of one man and several disguises. At least, that would be my guess. One man snatches a pocketwatch, sneaks into the next compartment before the theft has been discovered, and while doing so, changes some small but vital detail in his garb so as to transform him from, say, a Chelsea 'toff' into a low-ranking office assistant."

"What change would that be?"

"Oh, perhaps removing a fancy cravat to reveal the simple tie behind it, putting on or removing a false moustache, wrapping a worn muffler around the neck – things like that."

"I see. This theory really does you credit, dear friend."

"Thank you, Holmes."

"It really is most creative."

I put down my beer. "You tend to talk like this just before you're about to criticise me."

"Do I? Well, it is not empty flattery simply to ease the blow. I really mean it. It is a creative theory."

"But…?"

"But… perhaps you fail to consider a few vital points."

"Let's have it."

"I am not suggesting that this notion of a chameleon-like pickpocket is unlikely. It would certainly be a worthy adversary for us, for he would have to be a most ingenious and skilled artisan. But why develop such an advanced technique and such accomplished skills and then only use them in one public house? Undoubtedly it is a more lucrative public house to operate in than most, but all the same. If it is as Winstanton says and the same man is present every night, then he can hardly operate anywhere else, considering the extensive preparations he has to make for his tranformation acts. And although I do believe a small change in appearance would impede identification by those who have only seen him in the corner of their eye, I hardly think that he would have been able to escape the watchful eyes of Gregson and his men. For that he would need an entire wardrobe, and where would he hide that? No, there are too many fallacies in this theory, thought-provoking though it is."

"Very well. I appreciate your honesty. I assume that you prefer not to speak yet?"

"I have my suspicions. But at the moment, let us satisfy ourselves by scrutinising Mr Winstanton's story. It is all very neat and tidy, is it not? It looks like a classic case of pickpocketing. The crowded public place, the mixing of social classes, the proverbial cry of 'Stop thief' and the dexterity bordering on invisibility. There is something about it that does not feel quite right."

Just at that moment, a fellow next to me pushed against me and accidentally spilled some wine on my coatsleeve. My patience was running out.

"Holmes, I don't like places like this. Let's go home."

"Just a moment, Watson. Let us find out as much as we can while we are here. Who knows, we might just witness the thief in action. Ah, here comes one of the barmen. Mr Burleigh, unless I am mistaken?"

The broad-shouldered man, who had been serving the customers with tireless energy while we had been talking, started to wipe the counter in front of us with a wet rag.

"Can I help you gentlemen?" His voice boomed like a mountain troll's.

"What are your thoughts on these recent thefts?" asked Holmes.

Burleigh smiled with one half of his mouth. "Well, it's a nuisance, isn't it? Especially when they steal from them toffs, cause they make such a row, and they suspect us barmen."

"But I understand that this pickpocket doesn't just steal from the rich."

"Oh no. In fact, it was just that one time that a Lord was robbed. All the other times it was ordinary gentlemen, like you and me."

This curious comparison made me laugh. Holmes sniffed. "But you have quite a distinguished clientele, don't you?"

"Oh yeah. Have a look over there, in the inner parlour. The man with the buttonhole. He's a member of parliament, he is. Of course, the upper rooms are closed tonight. When they are open you can see one honourable member after another climbing those stairs."

"But our mysterious pickpocket has not seen fit to infiltrate that gathering?"

"Apparently not. Which is very lucky indeed for Mr Winstanton. If that occurred, he would be in trouble."

"How so?" I asked.

"They say he has a lot of fancy friends and many respected people have invested money in this venture."

"Really?" I said. "Who?"

"I'm afraid I couldn't tell you, sir. It may be just a rumour, but Mr Winstanton is up there, every night, sucking up to the well-to-do."

"I understand," said Holmes. "Well, thank you, Mr Burleigh. It was nice talking to you."

And just as I was starting to enjoy my beer, Holmes dashed off, out into the corridor, leaving me no option but to follow him.

"Are we finished here at last?" I queried.

"Not yet. Let us get an idea of the layout of the place before we leave."

Holmes started to walk down the corridor through which we had entered. Then he dashed here and there, in and out of the various compartments, quicker than I had time to react. I followed him into the front rooms, where the noise was unbearable and the crowds impenetrable, and then into the other corridor, leading into an identical series of rooms on the other side of the counter. The place was an absolute maze, and after a few minutes, I was almost completely disoriented, and satisfied myself by following in Holmes' footsteps without trying to get my bearings. When Holmes had scurried around long enough, however, he claimed to be content, and we could leave. I had the feeling that the Princess Louise was the type of public house that is very popular for a while, and during that time infernally crowded and noisy, until it falls out of favour and then is forgotten. My taste is more towards the quieter and more perpetual taverns that do not try so hard to attract business, like the Alpha Inn, for instance, which Holmes and I once had the opportunity to visit, and which lay not far from the Princess Louise.

On the cab ride home, Holmes was silent and I allowed him to remain so. Our night out had left me rather tired. He only said one thing to me, as we approached Baker Street.

"Did you notice, Watson, that the curtains at the Princess Louise were made of provencal velvet?"

"No, I did not."

"It is a very expensive type of velvet. I have only seen it once before."

"Where?"

"At Buckingham Palace."

And then the cab stopped, and Holmes climbed out.

When I came down to breakfast the next morning, Holmes had already gone out. It gave me time to ponder about the previous evening over my morning coffee, and to try and tie together some of the loose ends in my head. I gathered from what Holmes had said that it was a bit strange for a pickpocket to focus his attention on just one public house, and yet, since it was such a distinguished one, this did not seem to me so very odd. Furthermore, I was still not convinced that this was not the work of a gang, and I struggled to recall the faces that we had seen in the bar during our visit, and speculated whether there was anything suspicious about them. I could, however, only call to mind one gentleman who had been standing at the bar just opposite to us, and thus framed by my field of vision throughout my conversation with Holmes. There was nothing very peculiar about his appearance, but for some reason, I concluded that he was out of place in that particular compartment. The men around him looked a bit better dressed and more well-kempt. It was just an impression, and I could not put my finger on just what it was that made me think this, but it was often like that when you noticed people in public. One could with exactitude pinpoint their social and geographical position almost in an instinct, but when asked to describe one's reasoning, it was impossible. I suppose it was what Holmes used to call "seeing without observing."

Holmes returned just before lunch, and he was in a cheerful mood.

"A fruitful morning, I see?" I said as I folded up my newspaper.

"Is my demeanour that obvious? I must learn to be more reticent in your company, or else my innermost thoughts might be visible on my face."

"Is that such a bad thing?"

"If only you knew, Watson. If only you knew."

We chuckled and Holmes took his place beside me by the fire.

"Yes, the morning has been quite fruitful. I have made some inquiries concerning Mr Winstanton and his business venture, and I have been to see Gregson to find out the identity of the pickpocket victims."

I shook my head. "I find it a bit strange that you should automatically direct your suspicions towards the publican and the victims of the robberies. Not all businessmen have illicit motives, and not all men of distinction have skeletons in their closets."

Holmes put his forefinger to his mouth and looked at me broodingly. "Watson. How would you react if you fell victim to a pocketpicking?"

"What do you mean? I would be distraught, of course. You know I'm a bit hard up at the moment."

"Yes, but what would your instantaneous reaction be?"

"I suppose I would call out."

"Call out?"

"Yes. 'Stop thief.' Or words to that effect."

"Yes. That is what we would say a pickpocket victim would do, is it not? We have it from *Oliver Twist*, don't we? When Oliver becomes the scapegoat for the Artful Dodger and the lynch mob is formed."

"Yes. Happens every day in this city."

"Don't you think that depiction is a little dated?"

"Well, the book is a few decades old. What are you driving at?"

"You and I can count ourselves lucky that we have never – touch wood – fallen victim to pickpockets, but for people who have not, it is difficult to comprehend just how one would react

81

to it. The common assumption is that you become frantic and shout 'Stop thief', and maybe that is how people did react in Dickens' time. But city people are different now. They are more subdued and discreet, for one, and what is more, if you lose something in a public house, would you automatically assume that you have been robbed? Some of these victims must have been intoxicated at the moment. Would they not suspect themselves of carelessness and be rather ashamed? It is just a thought, but when Winstanton said that all of the victims had shouted out in the same manner, it made me suspicious."

"Suspicious of what?"

"And then there is the question of the Lord."

"You mean the one who was robbed? His name was in the morning paper."

"So the press have got hold of the affair now, have they? How very careless of Gregson."

"Lord Logan, was it?"

"Yes. His presence in this business made me wary from the moment I heard of it."

"Why? The place seems to be frequented by many men of his class."

"Yes. Which is why it is strange that only one such illustrious gentleman should figure in this whole affair, while the other victims are all common-or-garden run-of-the-mill sort of men. Why waste time on picking poor men's pockets when there are rich men about?"

"I suppose you have a point."

"Now, last night our presence must have deterred the culprits, but tonight we shall be there in disguise, and hopefully have our hands on this gang once and for all."

"Gang? But Holmes, you said this was not the work of a gang!"

"I said it was not the work of a pickpocket gang. But it is the work of a gang."

"I don't understand."

"All will be revealed this evening. I seem to remember you speaking a few days ago of some old suits that you wished to dispose of. If you could retrieve the shabbiest and most worn of those suits, we shall soon be at the Princess Louise, posing as a couple of down-at-heel bookkeepers."

Apart from my worn suit – which had large and visible moth holes on the sleeve to which Holmes replied with a "Marvellous, Watson" – Holmes supplied me with an uncomfortable and itchy false beard to wear on our pub visit. I could not help but feel ridiculous, but Holmes put on a pair of round spectacles and a small waxed moustache which more than surpassed me in silliness, and so I was satisfied. When we arrived at the pub it was half past six and the interior was already brimming with people. Before we entered, though, Holmes led me aside to a dark passageway a few yards from the front of the pub, where a gathering of men was hiding in the shadows. As we approached them, I recognised one of them as Inspector Gregson and the rest as uniformed policemen.

"Is everything ready?" asked Holmes.

"Absolutely," said Gregson with the confidence reserved for the voices of police officers.

"Perfect. You know the signal. Now it is only for Watson and me to mix with the crowd. Come, Watson."

I understood from this intermission that Gregson and his men were standing ready to rush in and apprehend the culprit if Holmes and I caught him redhanded, and saw no need to ask Holmes about it, but I was unsure of how our time would be spent until that moment.

"It is perfectly simple, Watson. Mingle with the customers and keep an eye open for anything that looks suspicious."

"And what would that be?"

"We will know that when we see it. This is for attracting Gregson's attention."

He handed me a police whistle, and was through the doors before I had time to protest.

Inside, the crowd was manic, and within seconds, I had lost sight of Holmes. I realised I had to adapt to the situation, so I brazed myself and dived into the mass of men before me. After a few minutes, I had managed to make my way to the counter, and ordered a glass of port. The man next to me gave me a look when the barmaid served me the drink, as if it was something exotic to him. I raised my glass to him and smiled. He responded by raising his beer tankard.

"I haven't seen you around here before," he remarked.

"No, I usually go to another place near here. But a friend suggested this place to me. Apparently a lot of influential people come here, which might be good if you're trying to make a name for yourself."

I was quite proud of this introduction, as it would lead into the topic of coming here for the purpose of acquiring wealth. But my drinking partner seemed only amused by my naïve attitude.

"Yeah, I've heard some men come here for that purpose. But they soon find out it is quite pointless. You see…" And he raised his hand and pointed across the counter to the inner rooms. "…they're over there, and we're over here. It's just like anywhere else, only here the walls between us are made of wood as well as money."

"The only thing that remains to do, I suppose, would be to steal their money." I realised that this remark was a bit too

84

direct, but I was struggling to find something suitable to say. The man just laughed, however, and raised his glass once more.

I looked about to see if I could spot Holmes, but the crowd was too dense. I took my glass and tried to squeeze away from the counter, only to find myself trapped in the middle of the room, surrounded by the backs of tailcoats and jackets. I stretched my neck to get an overview and heard a mumbled outcry from another part of the establishment, soon followed by the sound of a police whistle. The moment had come! A theft had taken place. People around me started to move about, and in this confusion I managed to get to the door and rushed out into the corridor. I continued in the direction of the sounds, which was the second compartment on the right-hand side of the bar. Gregson and his men were there already, and Holmes was standing next to a stout man in a brown billycock, who was talking very loudly.

"This is an outrage, Inspector! How appropriate that you were here to see this. Only a few days ago, a friend of mine was robbed in this very establishment, and now I come here only to become the victim of the same crime. Surely there is something amiss with this place!"

The inspector implored him to calm down and explain what had been stolen from him.

"My watch and chain. A gold chain, it was."

"And do you have any notion of how long ago the theft occurred, sir?"

"I checked the time only a few minutes ago."

Gregson looked at Holmes, who smiled back.

"I think you can arrest this man, Gregson," he said and laid his hand on the man's shoulder.

"What?" exclaimed the man. "I am the victim, sir, whoever you are, and you should make efforts to apprehend the culprit."

"There is no culprit," replied Holmes.

"No culprit? What poppycock is this?"

"There is no culprit, because you never had a watch on you. At least not since you came into this public house twenty minutes ago."

"What are you implying?"

By this time, Mr Winstanton had come into the room and was observing the scene with much interest.

"Yes, Holmes," he said. "What are you implying?"

"Mr Winstanton, your establishment is not the hunting ground for a gang of pickpockets. It is the place of action for a gang of wrongful accusers, like this gentleman here."

"Wrongful accusers?"

"They are in the employ of one of your great competitors, and have been ordered to come here and deter customers by spreading the false rumour that this is a notorious haunt for pickpockets. They number three or four men, at least, but their performances are a bit flawed. For instance, it never occurred to them that pickpockets would only target the richest customers in a place as this. This gentleman would hardly be able to afford a gold watch-chain. Instead, they thought it best to make it seem that the pickpockets were everywhere. The only illustrious victim in this whole affair – Lord Logan – does not exist."

The man in the brown hat was silent, at last, and Gregson's men escorted him out of the premises.

"But who would wish to do this, Mr Holmes?" said Winstanton.

"If we could talk privately for a moment," said Holmes, "I will explain as much as I can."

Winstanton brought us back into a small office next to the kitchens, where he fell into a rickety chair.

"Mr Winstanton," began Holmes, "you know that you are in a very vulnerable position. This venture has been a large investment for you, and you have sought help from the very highest of circles. But the pub business is a seedy business at heart, and creating such a lavish public house can be very provocative. So it was quite clear to me, when I started to get a picture of your situation, that you are a likely target for acts of sabotage or attempts to create a scandal. Finding out who commissioned these men to come into your pub and claim to have been pickpocketed will be difficult, of course, but whoever it is, they will find out that their scheme has been exposed. I advise you to be wary of similar actions in the future."

"Mr Holmes, I am extremely grateful to you. It seems to me that you never fell for this scheme in the first place."

"I had my suspicions. When you mentioned that all of the victims had called out in just the same manner, it appeared curious to me. We think that people are very predictable and instinctive in moments of crisis, but human nature is more complex than that. Now, if you will excuse us, Watson and I wish to get out of these ridiculous clothes as soon as possible."

"Of course, of course. There is just one more thing, Mr Holmes."

"Yes?"

"In what way is my wife deceitful? And how do you know?"

Holmes stopped in the doorway. "She kisses you on the cheek every morning, does she not?"

"Yes. How can you tell?"

"Because she leaves a few hairs on the shoulder of your jacket every time she does so, and they are hairs that have been dyed. I don't think her deception goes any further than that, but yesterday when I was in the dark as to why you had called for us, I guessed that her habit of dyeing was indicative of a more profoundly deceptive personality. I was wrong."

Mr Winstanton smiled. "I'm glad that even you can be wrong, Mr Holmes."

The Adventure of the Tooting Pyramid

There were many issues in connection with the mystery of Albany Place that were never cleared up at the time of its occurrence, and which have many times since made me think that I should communicate my own perspective on the matter to the reading public. I have hesitated in doing so only due to my respect for the people involved and my reluctance to evoke the painful image of Miss Landseer, the reclusive spinster, and the way she sat in her large armchair, bound to it by chains of fate. The reason I have finally picked up my pen to recall the details of the case is a most heartwarming letter from Miss Brill, the old woman's young companion and live-in maid, asking me to make public my version of the story so that Miss Landseer's honour might be restored. Miss Brill, who cared so selflessly for the old woman in the last years of her life, awoke my feelings of sympathy just as much as her employer did, and I am glad to present this account as a tribute to the strength of these two women and the model of humanity that their life together comprised.

It all began on a dreary day in September, when Holmes, after a hiatus of contact for a couple of weeks, sent me a spontaneous telegram inviting me to dine with him. My wife was entertaining some female friends that evening, so she readily consented to my absence, and, having seen off the last patient of the day, I took a hansom to Piccadilly where Holmes was waiting for me in a secluded booth at the Criterion. He looked delighted to see me, and I was glad to have caught him in a cheery mood.

"You arrived at just the critical moment, Watson! Have a seat, old boy, and take a discreet look at that waiter over there. I believe he is new here and from the way he casually carries those trays of wine glasses, he wishes to impress his new employer with his ease of comportment. His lack of experience is noticeable in the small details, however, for he is a bit too casual now and then, and he almost spilled some wine on a lady's dress two minutes ago. It is only a matter of time before a serious accident occurs."

Holmes had hardly finished his sentence before the wine glasses on the young waiter's tray started to glide as he swung round a table, and one by one they crashed to the floor. The sound was drowned out by the constant murmur from the dinner guests, but several of the closest diners were spattered by wine, and a gentleman quickly rose to scold the overconfident waiter. Holmes turned away from the commotion and glanced at me with one of his imperceptibly penetrating looks.

"I trust you are well, Watson? Jenkins back with another of his imagined maladies, is he?"

Philip Jenkins was one of my regular patients, a man of thirty-five who was in excellent health besides suffering from a most unrelenting hypochondria, and he would visit my practice at least once a month asking me to examine some ache or other that he fancied was a symptom of serious illness.

"Jenkins did see me today, yes. How could you tell?"

"You once told me about his curious habit of putting his tie-pin in your lapel when he unbuttons his shirt for you to listen to his heartbeat."

"Yes?"

"This time he has forgotten his tie-pin."

I looked down on my lapel and, lo and behold, there was Jenkins' tie-pin where he had left it a few hours earlier. I laughed at this foresight, but let it sit there so that I would be reminded to send it back to him at the earliest opportunity.

"Yes, well. I have been rather busy these past few days, if that is a reasonable excuse for my absent-mindedness."

"Do not feel ashamed, my boy. Absent-mindedness is an unavoidable consequence of professional success. I am only too glad that your practice is thriving."

"You hardly get absent-minded when your practice is thriving," I quipped.

Holmes took a few puffs on his cigar, obviously trying to hide a contented smile. "My mind is never absent. That is my curse."

The last remnants of the broken wine glasses were now swept up, and the diners at the other end of the room had resumed their pleasant dinner conversations. The inexperienced waiter, however, had vanished from the scene, and I sympathised for a second with his unfavourable confrontation with the restaurant manager that was most likely taking place in the kitchen. I forgot him once Holmes and I started to converse on sundry topics, and it was not until we had enjoyed a delicious meal involving guinea-fowl and trifle that he mentioned to me the real reason behind his invitation.

"I am due to go out to Tooting in a few minutes. I have received a pleading letter from a poor young woman, and her appeal is too pathetic to ignore."

"What does it concern?"

"As far as I can ascertain, it concerns loneliness, melancholy, lack of love, and defencelessness – matters that, judging from their occurrence in people's lives, are trivial and mundane, but which our time seldom takes enough of an interest in to broach. There is neither scandal, drama nor adventure in these topics, only the drawn-out smouldering tragedy of people who are moderately unfortunate, and thus will never warrant the charity of the Salvation Army."

"It sounds positively deplorable, Holmes. Although I must say I am a bit surprised to see you taking an interest in something based on sympathy."

There was a twitch in the side of Holmes' mouth that could be interpreted as both amusement and ache. **(Nice touch)**"You do not think me sympathetic?"

"Of course I do. But you have said yourself that it is the rational challenge and not the human aspect that draws you to your cases. Humans are mere factors in a problem, I think were your words."

"Did I really say that? Hm, well, I am an odd sort, am I not?"

"You mean you have altered your opinion?"

"Not quite, but I am surprised that I was so categorical in my statement. Perhaps we may attribute it to the folly of youth. Now I would say that the domain of ratiocination does not stop at the threshold of human passion. The emotions are also subject to the laws and systems of logic, and the close study of the minutest of details in an individual's inner life will reveal the most fascinating patterns of cogent structures. I have always considered both the rational and emotional side of the human mind in my methods, but for a long time I struggled to reconcile the two. I devoted a paragraph to this problem in my article 'The Book of Life', if you recall."

"This sounds more like you," I commented.

"I strive for consistency, my dear Watson. Now then, will you accompany me to Tooting?"

"Am I permitted to read this letter of yours?"

"After we have left. I prefer that you base your decision upon your loyalty to me rather than your sympathy for a woman you have never met."

"Then I will be more than glad to come with you, if I can be of service."

Holmes patted me on the shoulder as he would an obedient child, we settled our bill, and stepped into one of the broughams that were waiting for fares outside the restaurant. Just as we were rattling down Waterloo Place in the direction of the river, Holmes produced an envelope from the inside pocket of his overcoat, and handed it to me. The letter was written in the neat and distinct style of someone who does not write very often, and read thus:

"Dear Mr Holmes,

I write to you on behalf of my employer, who is in great need of your help. Miss Dorothy Landseer is an old spinster and invalid. I have nurtured for her and cared for her since I was a young girl, first as a hired companion, and successively as a loving friend, which is why I wish to give her the assistance she requires and deserves. I have heard of your accomplishments and your habit of assisting those unfortunates who are otherwise unable to remunerate an external adviser, and if anyone can help my poor mistress, it is you. As she is old and infirm, we beg that you pay us a visit at your soonest available moment. The matter is most pressing and troubling.

Yours faithfully,
Miss Constance Brill
Albany Place, Tooting."

"What do you say, Watson?" said Holmes as I looked up from the letter.

"It is certainly pleading and piteous, but I cannot see how it has attracted your interest. You must receive dozens of letters like this each week."

"I do indeed. Only the other day I was asked by the Crown Prince of Denmark to help him retrieve a lost terrier, but the whole case was so obvious from his letter, that it only required a brief telegram to resolve the matter. Here we have something more promising, however. A well-composed although slightly awkward-sounding letter from a woman whose modesty seems to sit at the heart of her personality. And yet she feels so passionately for her employer that she mobilises the strength to write to Sherlock Holmes, the famous investigator, to ask for assistance. This Miss Landseer is her whole world. She probably meets very few other people, and so the bond between these two women, presumably separated in age by several decades, has grown exceedingly strong. If there is no interesting problem at the heart of this, there is a most fascinating relationship to be studied at close range."

"I agree with you. But how can you be so sure that the relationship is such a strong one? Certainly this Miss Brill seems to care for her mistress, but there is nothing unusual about that."

Holmes took the letter and held it up close to his eyes.

"I have made a chemical examination of this paper at Baker Street, and there is reason to believe that the letter has been written on a dressing table. Upon the backside of the paper are traces of face powder and salicylic acid. The face powder is of a fabrication that has only just recently come into circulation, which suggests that it is the powder of a young woman, for an old one would surely use the trusted make that she has been using for decades. But when we add to this the little blotches of salicylic acid noticeable on one corner of the

94

paper, a medication that is commonly used to prevent rheumatic pains, the presence of an old person in the same household is apparent. That they make use of the same dressing table for what are rather personal businesses to me indicates a very close relation between the two."

"I was not aware that you have made women's face powder a subject of your research."

"My dear Watson, I cannot limit myself to varieties of cigarette ashes and moustache wax. If you look in my bookshelf, you will see a number of well-thumbed copies of the yearly catalogue from Derwent's Lady's Emporium. And, as you know, I have on several occasions put my knowledge of the female toilet to practical use."

"And with some success in the opposite sex, as I recall."

"Yes, yes. But how do you find my deductions?"

"Reasonable, I suppose."

"I see no other explanation to account for these concurrences. And so the main mystery at this point is not what Miss Brill is referring to in her letter, but the imaginary quandary that has taken shape in her mind from mixing the actual problem with her impassioned sympathy for her charge. It will be quite a challenge to separate the one from the other."

As we rattled southwards, I began to get infected by Holmes' enthusiasm, and was fascinated by his ability to extricate the enticing aspects of a case that, on the surface, looked commonplace and a little slight. When Holmes was in this mood, there was indeed very little that he could not cultivate an interest in, and I had seen him exercise this enthusiasm on everything from the construction of railway engines to the motets of Lassus. In due course, we arrived at the dispersed and slightly unfashionable suburb of Tooting, a place where few people with a wish to make a name for themselves would choose to reside for very long. I pondered over the fate that had caused a decrepit old lady to end up in such an odd corner of the outer fringe of suburbs, but when we approached Albany Place, I realised that the erection of the house predated with some years the erection of the suburb. It was surrounded on all sides by a wild and unattended garden, and a thick wisteria covered a large part of the exterior, with the exception of a slim turret rising from the heart of the edifice, giving it a peculiar tapered shape.

"Someone has taken great care to draw and build a characteristic house, which someone else has taken great care to neglect," mused Holmes as we walked up the front path.

The ground floor of the building had barely any windows, and the two small stained-glass windows on either side of the front door did not show anything of the interior. We rang the door bell, having concluded that the door was too thick to allow the sound of knocking to penetrate it.

"A ramshackle old house and impenetrable fortress at the same time?" Holmes commented.

We were let in by a discreet and courteous young woman, looking quite plain in a muslin tea-gown and braided hair, but with a lustrous face that made us feel welcome.

"I received your wire forewarning us of your arrival, Mr Holmes. We are most grateful that you have found time to look in on us."

"I try to find time for every pressing matter that comes in my way."

"And the matter is certainly most pressing. I am Miss Constance Brill, companion of Miss Dorothy Landseer of the Dorset Landseers. I can see from your puzzled faces that you wonder how such an illustrious lady has ended up in this remote corner of the metropolis. It is a long story, but as I doubt that Miss Landseer is willing to tell it herself, I will say that her family was once very wealthy and renowned, supplying no less than three peers in the reign of George III, but due to an epidemic of tropical fever that was brought home from Africa by Miss Landseer's explorer cousin, her whole family perished within months, and Dorothy, who was then away in Switzerland attending a girls' school, was the only member of the family left untouched by the dreadful illness. There was only very little for her to inherit, however, as her father had been heavily in debt at the time of his demise, and it was only enough for her to purchase this house, which was already out of fashion at that time, and had been abandoned by its previous owners. Here she has lived in solitude for the past forty years, and I have been with her for fifteen years, caring for her. Now she is past ninety, and has not long to live, but she is much troubled by the events of the past few weeks, which she will tell you about herself."

"And what about yourself?" asked Holmes just as Miss Brill was about to take us further inside the house.

"Myself? I'm sure I don't know what you mean."

"What is your background, Miss Brill? Why have you stayed with your mistress for so long?"

"Oh, there is precious little to tell about me, and I do not see that it is relevant in this matter, but if you must know I was born and raised only a few miles from here, and started coming here as a girl delivering groceries from my parents' shop. Then Miss Landseer's housekeeper passed away, and I was approached with the offer. At that time it was the only prospect for my future that I had encountered, and I gladly accepted. The reason why I stayed for so long is that I grew increasingly fond of Miss Landseer, as my letter indicated, and after a few years I had no interest in changing my life."

"But no suitors? No other offers?" I queried. "For such an delightful young woman there must have been numerous prospects?"

"My work with Miss Landseer has made me a free woman. Much freer than I would have been with a husband, or in a regular household. We live together as friends."

"I see."

Her face was motionless when she spoke these honest words, and her placid confidence made it impossible for me to question the situation further. She escorted us through the hallway, a dark and gloomy interior dominated by oak panelling. We walked across a large Persian rug, up four steps, and then through a door that led into a rather more pleasant drawing room. By the side of a blazing fire that made the room almost a bit too hot even in this rough weather, sat a small and unassuming creature, at first just a vague movement within the depths of a large wing chair, made visible by the flicker of the flames, but as we moved forward a couple of wringing hands and a pale wrinkled face on the end of a strangely conical head, rather like the face of a sloth, became discernible. The only sound that reached our ears apart from that of the crackling logs, was the sound of the smooth ancient skin on her hands as she wrung them, over and over again.

Miss Brill invited us to sit on two smaller armchairs placed in front of her mistress as if only for our benefit, as she placed herself on a simple footstool slightly behind her employer.

"Welcome to Albany Place, gentlemen," said the old woman in an unexpectedly youthful voice. "I wish I could have welcomed you as guests a few decades ago, when the world was different and this house was more alive than it is now. But we must all face our destiny with our heads held high, and I cannot say that fate has treated me unfairly. I accept my lot and

98

have no complaints. I am alone and the world has grown too large for me, but I am blessed enough to have my dear Connie by my side, and together we lead a pleasant enough existence. The events of these recent days, however, have unnerved me, and I wish only to make heads or tails of them so that I may recover my peace of mind."

"Lay your matter before us," said Holmes, "and spare us no details, however trifling or grotesque."

"Very well, Mr Holmes. But before I explain to you my reason for summoning you, I feel I ought to explain some things about our life here. Albany Place was built many years ago by an artist, who designed the curious structure that you see today. But he only lived here for two years before dying from a heart attack, and I bought the house after it had been deemed unfashionable and nobody but rats and pigeons had made use of it for some years. Now, however, I am too old and infirm to be able to enjoy the house in its entirety. I have no money to employ a staff of servants to keep the house in good order, nor would it be necessary for me to do so, as I am unable to climb the stairs, and am committed to live in this room and an adjoining bedroom that has been converted for my benefit from the old smoking room. Connie has taken up residence in the kitchen maid's old room, but we have long since disposed of the conventional spatial and social divisions between master and servant. You must understand, therefore, that the rest of the house is virtually abandoned, and neither I nor Connie have been upstairs for years.

"This state of things has bearing on the matter in hand. It began a week and a half ago. Connie and I retire late every evening, as we enjoy sitting by the fire, chatting and doing needlework. The evening in question, we were sitting here, when suddenly Connie said to me that she could hear a strange noise. We sat in silence for a while, and I tried to distinguish it myself, but was unable to do so with my impaired hearing. Connie said it was a faint but consistent creaking, didn't you, Connie, dear?"

Miss Brill leaned forward. "Yes. It was barely audible, but as it was so consistent, it was impossible not to notice it after a while."

"I naturally attributed it to rats," continued Miss Landseer, "as I suspect there are quite a few in the upper regions of the house, and after a few minutes we forgot the matter and the sound seemed to disappear. But the following evening, there it was again. And this time, Connie went upstairs to investigate."

The old woman handed the tale over to her companion with a sweeping gesture.

"The sound was coming from somewhere in the upper regions of the house," Miss Brill said. "I have actually only been up the stairs on one or two occasions during my years here, and then only out of curiosity. In those instances, I was halted at the top of the first flight of stairs by my own fear, for, being an old and deserted house, it has many strange sounds that can make even the boldest of men tremble. I also think that this fear has grown in me since those first ventures up the stairs. On the occasion in question, though, I told myself that it would be foolish to fear whatever would meet me at the top of those stairs, and tried to ignore any fantasies that would run through my mind. When I had come to the top of the first flight of stairs, the sound was more distinct. It was a continuous scratching, and reminded me of the sound of someone scratching off paint from a wall. For a moment I paused, and considered the possibility that this sound came from inside my head and that I was going insane. But just then, the scratching became more frenetic and loud, and it was clear to me that it came from the first room on the left, an old bedchamber. I carefully trod the creaking floorboards up to the door and pushed it open. A bang, as of something dropping, could be heard, and the scratching ceased, only to be supplanted by a series of clanks and creaks. The source of all these sounds was undoubtedly the window, and I rushed up to it, my fear now overpowered by a relentless curiosity. I reached it just in time to see a figure emerging from the shadows of the lower outside wall and run across the lawn into the bushes."

"We were convinced," continued Miss Landseer, "from what Connie had seen, that we had been the victims of a burglary attempt. We summoned the police the next day, and they examined the upstairs room and the wall leading up to the window, but could not find any clear signs of an intruder. The drainpipe was loose in a couple of places and the wisteria had been pulled at, but there was nothing that could be separated from the rest of the damage on the exterior that are only to be attributed to lack of maintenance. It was apparent from the countenance of the policeman that he considered our complaint unfounded, and he suggested that rats was the cause."

"But only two days later," said Miss Brill, "the sound returned."

"This time, however, it was a different sound," Miss Landseer added.

"Different?" I said. "How so?"

"It had changed from a scratching to a banging," replied Miss Brill. "It was hardly a very loud banging, but enough to startle us. We first heard it in the middle of the night, and it woke us both up. I went up to investigate once more, but this time it came from even higher up, and so I had to climb two flights of stairs. The second floor is quite small, owing to the curious dwindling shape of the building, as I am sure you noticed upon arriving. There is barely a corridor, only four rooms entered through a diamond-shaped hallway. I fancied the sound was coming from the second door, and carefully opened it. In the moonlight that came in through the window, I could see the contours of furniture covered with old bed linen and a moth-eaten stuffed fox on a tabletop, but there was no movement. Just then, I was startled by the sound of the banging starting again just behind me. I turned around and concluded that it came from within the fourth room. The door creaked as I opened it, and I managed to glance into the dark room quick enough to see what I imagined to be a shadow sweeping past the window. I gathered that there was someone outside again, and this time I wanted to intercept him. I ran down the stairs as fast as I could and out of the front door. The window I had seen him in was on the north side of the house, and I positioned myself below it to catch him as he came down. But he was not there. Was I too late? It could not be. Climbing down the exterior of the house from such a height would take at least five minutes, and I had been down in thirty seconds. There was only one explanation. He had managed to get inside. So I ran inside once more, and went up to the first floor to listen for sounds. I could hear someone walking above me. What was I to do? We were only two defenceless women in an old house, the size of which became evident to me for the first time. Then I remembered the hunting rifle that hangs above the fireplace in our drawing room." She pointed at a very old and surely quite useless weapon hanging from a few nails. "I entertained no illusions to the point that it would be able to fire this antique, but I went down and took it all the same, thinking that it could be used to intimidate the intruder.

"I went up to the second floor, holding the weapon before me. I saw at once that the door to the fourth room had been opened, but there was no sign of the burglar. He must have made his way down to the first floor while I went down for the rifle, I thought, and as I came down to the first floor landing, I could see a silhouette running away down the corridor.

"'Halt!' I shouted, and it must have been the excitement of the moment, for without meaning to, I pulled the trigger of the rifle, and to my great astonishment and alarm, a shot went off! There was a sound as of shattering glass, and I think I must have broken a window at the far end of the corridor. It was too dark up there to see clearly, but I think the intruder took advantage of the broken window, and climbed out that way."

Miss Landseer put a friendly hand on Miss Brill's knee. "Connie scared them away," she said with a tinge of pride.

"This is a most curious business," I remarked. "Who would want to break into a house that looks as dilapidated as this? Or is there anything of value in your possessions that might attract a thief?"

"Not in the least," said Miss Landseer. "I have lived on very little money since I was forced to settle my father's debts."

"All the more strange," I said, "because that precludes the eventuality that the burglar knew who was living here, and had set his eye on some well-known heirloom of yours. Don't you think it strange, Holmes?"

"I do, but it is hardly without sense. There is at least some logic in the way the burglar tried to force the weak parts of the house – the run-down upper floors – as the ground floor has a very thick front door that would take time to break in through, and the only windows, as I gather, are in the back rooms that you use as private quarters. He would not be able to get into the ground floor without running the risk of waking you up. The venture is helped, furthermore, by the shape of the house, making it quite easy to climb the exterior. It has numerous ledges and holes suitable for grabbing when you climb, and taken together with the wisteria, it means you do not even have to be very agile to be able to scale the wall. But tell me, has there been further attempts since this one?"

"There was one more," said Miss Landseer, "about four days later. This time, he seems to have given up the moment he heard Connie going up the stairs. I think he tried to force another one of the first-floor windows, but without success."

Holmes jumped in his seat. "Ha! This run-down house seems more solid than most of its kind."

"It is a very sturdy construction, Mr Holmes."

"Yes, but so, my experience tells me, is the perseverance of burglars. And have there been no further incidents since that time? This must have been several days ago."

The two women exchanged glances.

"No, Mr Holmes," said Miss Landseer, "there has been nothing. We were deeply unsettled by the events, however, and Connie wrote her letter to you the day after the last attempt. We live here in solitude and tranquillity, and do not take such intrusions lightly."

Holmes placed his forefinger across his lips. "But surely, Miss Landseer, you receive visitors to this day."

"How can you say?"

"Because the chairs that Watson and I are sitting in have both been standing here for at least a few weeks, judging from the deep imprint they have made in the rug. One of them is surely for Miss Brill, but what about the other one?"

The women looked at each other again, this time with a smile.

"You are quite right," said Miss Landseer, "we do receive a visitor. Mr Hutchinson, a retired furniture salesman who recently moved into one of the smaller houses down the road. He knocked on our door four nights ago, wishing to acquaint himself with his new neighbours."

"He was so utterly charming," added Miss Brill, "that I could hardly refuse to let him in."

"Yes," Miss Landseer smiled, "we became quite fond of Mr Hutchinson, and he has come back to chat with us over a cup of coffee every evening since then. But that is another matter entirely, and our business with you was the burglar."

Holmes studied the old woman's placid face.

"You will forgive me for prying, I'm sure, but I am fascinated by gentlemen who manage to carry themselves with such irresistible charm. I am quite a student of charm, is that not so, Watson?"

I had no idea what he was rambling about, but he gave me no time to answer him.

"Just what made this man so appealing to you?" he asked.

"He is an impeccable gentleman, Mr Holmes," replied Miss Landseer.

There was a suggestion of impatience in her voice, as if she indicated that the gentleman who sat before her was less than impeccable. I had to bite my lip to keep from laughing.

"He is so unselfish," said Miss Brill. "He always insists upon seeing himself out when he leaves, and will not go until he has made sure we are continuing with our needlework, and that his visit has not interrupted us too much."

Miss Brill started to giggle a bit, and her mistress smiled approvingly.

"It must be most satisfying to make an acquaintance after so long in isolation," remarked Holmes.

"As I am chained to this wretched chair most of my time," said Miss Landseer, "it certainly is a blessing to be offered some diversion. I am glad this confinement has not driven me insane, although one does develop one's quirks. For instance, I have grown accustomed to hearing Connie walk around in the house, and from the sound of her steps I can determine just where she is. And when Mr Hutchinson leaves, I can hear him walk out of that door, down the four steps in the foyer and then the muted sound of his shoes as he crosses the Persian rug just before he goes through the door. It is as if I was blind and had developed acute hearing. Do you know, I was disconcerted yesterday, when Mr Hutchinson left us."

"How so?"

"Well, it is a most curious thing. I can hear so clearly the sound as he walks down those four steps. There are five distinct footfalls, one for each of the steps and then one as he comes down on the wooden floor. But yesterday there were only four!" She laughed to herself. "Can you imagine? As if he vanished into thin air before coming down the steps."

"I doubt the gentlemen are interested in these fancies, Miss Landseer," said Miss Brill. "Perhaps you prefer to make an examination of the rest of the house?"

"I was just about to suggest it," said Holmes, and rose. "But there is no need for you to escort us. Watson and I will manage on our own."

I cannot claim to have been enthusiastic about this venture after hearing the ladies' ghoulish story, but with Holmes at my side I was prepared for anything, and I was rather curious about this strange house. Climbing the stairs to the first floor also gave Holmes and me a good opportunity to air our thoughts on the case.

"I must admit to feeling a bit doubtful to this business, Holmes," I confessed. "In the end, it is but a common case of burglary. And as regards the eccentric aspects of it, I am sure you would find similar characteristics if you scrutinised any break-in up close."

"I see your point, Watson. There is perhaps more to be had for the student of curious interpersonal entanglements than for the student of grotesque crimes, but it is the obstinacy of this burglar that intrigues me. A burglar who seems to have set his mind on penetrating a house that to the uninitiated only looks like a deserted ruin, and to the initiated is only the home of two impoverished ladies. If a burglar scoured this area looking for suitable targets, he would find numerous other houses that from the outside look much more rewarding. This leads one to think that the burglar knows of something in this house worth taking. But there is nothing! Miss Landseer had a cracked teacup at her elbow, and her dress had been mended several times. Despite her illustrious past, this is not the home of wealthy people."

We looked into rooms that had not been touched for decades, searching for traces of burglary or for something worth stealing, but the only signs of intrusion were mouse droppings. I inspected one of the windows, and found that the hooks were so thick as to be almost impossible to loosen.

"No wonder he was struggling to break in."

"Yes, it is ironic, is it not? An impenetrable ruin. The window frames are exceedingly thick and strong, much like the front door. The house seems at one point to have been built to deter burglars."

"No need for such safety anymore. Oh Holmes, this is useless. There is nothing here."

"I agree with you. Nothing at all."

"What are we to do, then?"

"I fear there is little we can do here now. I need to make some enquiries, and perhaps this will shed light on the only valuable clue that Miss Landseer provided us with."

"Only one valuable clue? And which is that?"

"The mystery of the fifth footfall."

Holmes and I descended the stairs and bade the two ladies farewell. As we came out into the street, Holmes instructed me to take a cab home and be reunited with my wife, while he took one to Baker Street. I tried to explain that we could easily share one, but he was most insistent, and I appreciated that he wished to stay behind for a while, dwelling on the problem. The following day, my practice did not keep me quite as busy as it had the day before, and I was given time to ponder the business of the previous evening. My theories moved in the direction of squatters rather than burglars, suspecting that perhaps some tramp had come upon the house, thinking it deserted, and then tried to get inside. This did not explain why he kept trying to break in after learning that the house was inhabited, but it is possible that this would not have bothered him. In any case, I felt that the tumbledown appearance of Albany Place was a vital clue in solving the matter.

My reflections had not advanced very far when I was handed a note at lunch. It was from Holmes, and it instructed me to go and join him in Tooting for the conclusion of the burglary business. My afternoon was free from appointments, and it was no strain for me to make a brief excursion. Holmes was waiting for me on a street corner as I came walking towards the house, and I was surprised to recognise on him the exact same clothes that he had worn when we had said goodbye the night before.

"Your suspicious look does you credit, Watson. I have indeed spent the night in this neighbourhood, which accounts for my slightly sullied attire. After we left Albany Place yesterday evening, I was convinced that any investigations in connection with this business must be carried out in the neighbourhood and as soon as possible. I therefore stayed behind after you had left, not wanting to involve you in my plans and deprive Mrs. Watson of the safe return of her husband."

"But what in God's name have you been doing all night?"

"My first order of business, as so often, was to visit the local public house. It is quite close by, called The Raven and Writing Desk, and its proprietor is a pleasant and most informative man who has been doing business in the area for the last forty years. He had some interesting things to tell me about Albany Place and its history. The unusual form of the house has awarded it the nickname of the Tooting Pyramid among the local inhabitants. I also spoke to one of the patrons of the bar, who happened to live next door to Mr Hutchinson. When I had satisfied my appetite for information, I went back to the house and positioned myself in a beech tree in the garden from where I had a good view of anyone who approached the house. I was not surprised to experience that the night passed in tranquillity, and my first port of call this morning was to summon Inspector Lestrade, who unwittingly has come in contact with this case from quite a different entry point. He supplied me with the last pieces of the puzzle, and I immediately sent for you so that you could be present for the last act."

"You mean you have cracked it?"

"Certainly. It was not such a great mystery, but it all hinged on one tiny little detail that most people would miss."

I could not get anything more out of him until we were back at Albany Place. Miss Brill once again escorted us into the drawing room where her mistress was sitting, just like the night before.

"Mr Holmes," she said with anticipation. "Am I right in thinking you have good news for us?"

"Yes and no, Miss Landseer."

"I don't understand."

"It will all be explained. But I prefer to give you my explanation with the help of a small demonstration. Could I ask you both to accompany me out into the hall?"

Miss Landseer looked vexed at this request.

"Is that absolutely necessary, Mr Holmes?" pleaded her loyal companion.

"I am afraid so," said Holmes unflinchingly.

Miss Brill assisted Miss Landseer in rising from her chair, and, with the aid of a cane and the support of both Miss Brill and myself, she managed to leave the room that otherwise was her domain. In the hall, Holmes stood before us, below the four steps that divided the room.

"Now then, Miss Landseer, you are absolutely certain that upon Mr Hutchinson's last departure, you only heard four steps and then nothing?"

"It is just as I told you." Miss Landseer seemed a bit impatient.

"Have you heard from Mr Hutchinson after that occasion?" asked Holmes.

"No, we have not."

"I understand. You will observe now that the Persian rug that lies here between the front door and the steps is placed about two and a half feet from the steps. Is that where it is usually placed?"

"Yes," said Miss Brill. "That is exactly where it always lies."

"Then would you permit me to conduct a small experiment?"

Holmes placed himself between the rug and the steps. He took hold of the end of the rug, and pulled it towards him, so that it reached all the way to the steps.

"Watson," he said. "Will you be so good as to walk in my direction?"

I did as he instructed, and walked down the steps and onto the rug. The sound of my shoes on the four steps made a clear sound that was contrasted by the almost complete silence that followed as I stepped onto the rug.

"Do you see?" said Holmes. "Four distinct footfalls, and then silence. Did it sound something like that, Miss Landseer?"

"It sounded exactly like that."

"Did any of you move the rug?"

"No," said Miss Brill. "The rug is never moved. I have never seen it lying that close to the steps."

Miss Landseer trembled as she firmly held onto her stick.

"What is the meaning of this, Mr Holmes?"

"I was trying to demonstrate, Miss Landseer, that when Mr Hutchinson was walking out of your house that last time, the rug must have been moved like this, to account for the absence of a sound."

"It could mean that, although I find it highly unlikely. I mean, why would it suddenly be moved, and then moved back?"

"That is precisely what we must find out."

Holmes stepped across the rug to the end closest to the door. Here, a large portion of the floor that had been covered by this old rug for years was suddenly revealed. Holmes fell down on his knees, and inspected this area. Within seconds, his hands had paused at one particular point, and then, to the astonishment of his audience, he opened a hatch in the floor, roughly the size of a dinner tray. Miss Landseer, by her own volition, staggered closer to be able to peer into the hole beneath it. The hatch covered a compartment a few feet deep, built into the floor like a wooden box. It was empty.

"Good God," whispered Miss Landseer. "I had no idea that was there. How did you know?"

Holmes stood up and brushed a considerable amount of dust from the knees of his trousers.

"I have been looking into the history of this house, Miss Landseer. The man who built it, a Mr Claude Quiller, was for a very brief time one of England's most sought-after portrait painters. He grew wealthy, and started to develop a tremendous fear of burglary, so that when he built this house, he made it into a fortress, with thick window frames and a front door that you cannot even knock on. His suspicions also prevented him from telling his friends and relatives where he kept his fortune hidden, and after his sudden death his family turned the house upside-down looking for it without success. The idea that the money was hidden in the house was abandoned, as was the house itself, and it fell into disrepair until you acquired it. The mystery of Quiller's fortune was forgotten until a most diligent burglar, whose real name we might never know, through meticulous research became certain that he had unravelled the secret, and was most determined to test his theory. First, he did it the old-fashioned way, by attempting to break into the house at night. This proved fruitless, for the inhabitants of the house were fiercer than he had reckoned with. From your stories, however, it was clear that the thief only climbed to the upper floors because they were easier to break into, but that his real interest lay down the stairs, where he tried to go before being stopped by Miss Brill's rifle. Exactly where on the ground floor he thought the treasure lay hidden became apparent to me when I understood the significance of the fifth footstep. You see, this burglar tried another method, and for this he required an accomplice. He would himself go into the house in disguise, posing as Mr Hutchinson, a new neighbour, and when he had gained the confidence of the two women, and sat chatting with them at length, his accomplice could sneak in through the unlocked door, open the hatch where the money was hidden, and run away with it undetected. Our thieves even had the patience to wait a few days until they had made sure that the two ladies had really fallen for his bluff. When the theft had actually taken place, however, Mr Hutchinson's accomplice must have forgotten to pull back the rug to hide the hatch. Luckily, Hutchinson had made his hosts stay behind in the drawing room when he left, so that he could make sure on his own that there were no traces of the intrusion, and this was when he walked across the misplaced rug and then pulled it back into its rightful place before leaving Albany Place, never to come back."

Miss Landseer was quiet, peering into Holmes' eyes as if she had been abused. "How can you possibly know all this?"

"I spoke with the landlord of your local, and with the man who lives next door to the house in which 'Hutchinson' and his accomplice moved two weeks ago, and from where they suddenly vanished the day after your last visit from them. I have also consulted the police in this matter, and they informed me that the two gentlemen who rented the house down the road match the description of two infamous burglars who they have been looking for for a long time. They were under the surveillance of the police, who lost track of them, however, about two days before they moved in as your neighbours. Where they have gone to now, with whatever they took from the secret hiding place in your floor, remains to be seen. If they keep up their meticulous and patient planning, we might not see them ever again."

"Goodness," said Miss Brill. "So you mean to say that there was a treasure underneath our hallway the whole time we have been living here?"

"Yes."

"And now it is stolen?" said Miss Landseer. "Stolen from under our very noses!"

"Look on it from a positive angle, Miss Landseer. You never knew that you had this treasure, so why mourn the fact that it is gone?"

Miss Landseer put on a cynical grin.

"Perhaps it would have been better if you were never summoned here to inform us of our loss."

"In that case, I must make amends, and do everything in my power to help the police in tracking the thieves."

We thus took our leave of the two ladies, who still seemed shocked by the lengthy explanation they had just received, and barely thanked us for our help.

"An attractive little mystery, eh, Watson?" said Holmes as we were walking down the street. "Incomprehensible when viewed from the perspective of Miss Landseer and her companion, but with a little outside information the whole thing was quite transparent."

"I suppose so," I said. "But how you managed to narrow it down to a hatch in the floor, I cannot fathom."

"I based my reasoning entirely on the factor of the absent fifth footstep. We have encountered numerous cases, have we not, that hinged on something commonplace that has always been there, but suddenly is not? I look for such details, because I know that they tend to lead to a solution. If there is aberration in the midst of the mundane, the contrast is more easily detected."

Holmes and I walked away from Albany Place in contentment of a satisfying solution, unaware of what proportions the case was to take. It appeared that a newspaperman had been listening to Holmes' interrogations at the public house, and, conjoining the snatches of conversation he had overheard with fragmentary information gained from some informant in the police force, he concocted a story claiming that Miss Landseer had purchased the house in complete awareness that it was the hiding place of the Quiller fortune, and had lived in luxury off the money since then, even hiring Sherlock Holmes to corroborate the hoax that the money had been stolen by burglars. These lies were most ardently refuted at the time, both by me in a letter to *The Times*, and by Inspector Lestrade in a public statement, but as the chances of catching the criminals diminished with each day so that no traces of them were found, and Miss Landseer herself seemed to prefer to let the matter rest, the false allegations of the gutter press were allowed to stand virtually unopposed. Now, several years later, the public might be prepared to absorb the finer details of the case and view it in its true light. Nothing was ever heard of the devious "Mr Hutchinson" and his accomplice again, although Holmes strongly believed that reports of similar crimes in New Jersey six months later contained strong indications of the same mind at work. An occasional correspondence with Miss Brill since our visit to Albany Place has assured me that the two women residing there lived on in the fashion they preferred until the peaceful demise of Miss Landseer two years later. I have been given to understand from the account of Miss Brill that her mistress spoke enthusiastically about Sherlock Holmes and his memorable visit to her house until her last days.

The Adventure of the Hobnailed Boots

The case of the six Napoleon busts which I have recounted previously in these annals, was, as my trusty readers might recall, a mystery of some momentum that had its beginnings in something seemingly trivial, brought to Sherlock Holmes' attention by Inspector Lestrade of Scotland Yard. Holmes' subsequent success in solving this case was met with much admiration from the good inspector, who proceeded by approaching Holmes in the following months with a number of similar trifles, expecting the consulting investigator to reveal their connection to some significant crime. Most of these cases, I am sorry to say, proved to be nothing more than the trifles they appeared to be at first sight. Among them were the amusing incident of the corn dolly, the slight but diverting case of the red-nosed pickpocket, and the affair of the bigamist Oliver Treadwell, who managed to keep three wives oblivious of each other's existence in different flats of one and the same house. But in this mostly unrewarding string of investigations, I retain in my records notes of one that proved much more consequential than was first suspected.

It began, as all of the cases mentioned above, with our receiving a visit from Lestrade, who was, at this time, in the habit of dropping by at Baker Street in the afternoons to enjoy a free cigar from Holmes' seemingly endless supply, which he eccentrically stored in the coal scuttle. Holmes questioned the unassuming little policeman on his recent work, ever eager to find a gem of a puzzle within the output of commonplace matters that made up the majority of the policework. On this occasion, Lestrade had been looking impatient from the moment he arrived, and it was apparent to me that he was enjoying the sensation of knowing something that Holmes did not know but would be very interested in.

"Do you know," he said after chatting with us for nigh on twenty minutes, "there is a small affair that has come my way recently which might be right up your street, Mr Holmes."

"And you are referring to the theft of your bicycle?" said Holmes.

Lestrade was distracted from the relish of his secret. "How the devil did you know about that?"

"I know that you are a keen cyclist in your leisure time, and the traces are usually apparent in the characteristic marks on your boots. But you have been wearing a new pair of boots on your two recent visits, and they lack the distinctive marks from the pedals. Thus, you have not been indulging in your favourite pastime for at least two weeks, and when a man is as passionate about something as you clearly are, one concludes that he has been robbed of this pleasure through circumstances that are beyond his control."

Lestrade leaned forward in his chair and touched the side of his left boot. "The blackguards took it straight from the driveway. The sheer nerve!"

"It was not my intention to remind you of sadder things," said Holmes. "You were about to tell us something."

"Indeed I was, and perhaps your keen eye concerning footwear will come in handy in this problem. It is a case of alleged assault reported at Hackney police station yesterday morning, and it only came to my attention by coincidence when I had business there today. Apparently, it concerns a Mr Montague Selwyn, a railway porter living locally, who, while walking home the night before, had been struck on the head with something heavy so that he lost consciousness immediately, and when waking up in the deserted alley where

118

the assault had taken place, learned that nothing had been stolen, except that his boots had been pulled off his feet and were nowhere to be seen. As the hour was late and he was close to his lodgings, he went home and did not report the theft until the following morning. A police constable accompanied him to the scene of the crime to investigate, but nothing could be ascertained. Mr Selwyn had neither seen nor heard anything strange prior to the attack, and could see no reason why anyone would want to run off with his boots. The robbery constitutes no great loss to him, as the boots in question were purchased at a second-hand clothes store for a small sum; small even for an impecunious labourer such as Mr Selwyn. The main reason why he reported the crime, he says, is his bafflement and more than wishing to retrieve the boots, he would like to know why the robbery was committed."

"What a curious story," I remarked. "It is the type of incident that you read brief notices of in the evening newspapers and then never hear the resolution. I expect things like that occur every day in this bustling metropolis."

"You would be surprised, Dr Watson," said Lestrade, "at all the singular occurrences that the police have to deal with. Some of them are merely strange and amusing, such as this one, but a great majority of them, I am sorry to say, are grotesque and illustrative of the basest aspects of human nature."

"Did the police make inquiries at the second-hand clothes dealer?" asked Holmes, whose gaze had not strayed from Lestrade during his narrative.

"I doubt it," said Lestrade. "Although the boots had been purchased not more than two weeks prior to the theft. But the whole thing is evidently some form of madness. I know, Mr Holmes, that I said so about the Napoleon bust business, but in that affair there was always a hint of something sinister, what with the violence of the deeds and the breakages. Here we have a man who commits an act of violence, I grant you, but only with one blow, and only to remove something that he cannot possibly make any money on. I advised the men to make a list of known escaped lunatics who might have been in the vicinity on that day."

"That sounds like a good strategy," I commented. "People who have taken leave of their senses often perpetrate the type of deeds you have described. On the spur of the moment, they swing something hard on the head of a passer-by without realising the strength of the blow. Seeing the result, this man was probably overcome with guilt, deterring him from striking again, and in his twisted logic the removal of the shoes was seen as some sort of conciliatory gesture. Or maybe he has an obsession in connection with footwear, and can be struck without warning by a strong impulse to steal the first pair that comes along."

"We are back to the *idée fixe* again, Dr Watson!" cried Lestrade in a mixture of enthusiasm and disappointment. "Is Watson right this time, Mr Holmes?"

"He might be," said Holmes, stroking his chin in contemplation. "I confess that the madness theory seems a bit more applicable here than in the Napoleon case. But I am reluctant to succumb to it, if only because the simplicity of it jars with my sense of aestheticism. After all, gentlemen, we must assume that a majority of people are sane and only a minority insane – at least to the point of stealing boots without reason. So based on that statistical assumption, we should consider other possibilities before seriously considering madness."

"But what are the other possibilities?" I asked.

"Aha!" Holmes raised his hands as if in triumph. "Let us dwell on the matter." With a bounce, he was out of his chair and had placed himself next to the blackboard that he kept on an easel in a corner next to the fireplace. He grabbed a bit of chalk in his hand and assumed the pose of an interrogating headmaster. "Now then, how many possible reasons for stealing a pair of boots off someone's person can we come up with?"

Lestrade and I looked at each other to try and surmise whether we should react with laughter or sincerity. But Holmes was perfectly serious, and he looked at us both with such intensity that I almost felt like I was headed for the dunce's chair.

"Well," mumbled Lestrade eventually, "the thief could have been the previous owner of the boots, and wanted to retrieve them for sentimental reasons. Perhaps his wife had sold them in a moment of rage, and he was so furious that he went out to track them down."

I could not help but chuckle slightly at Lestrade's theory, which he himself did not seem to believe in.

He peered at me. "I am struggling here, Doctor! Do you have any suggestions?"

Holmes dutifully wrote "1) Previous owner" on the blackboard, then turned to me with an expectant face.

"Uh, er… well, there is something of the Blue Carbuncle in this, is there not? Maybe someone has hidden something inside the boots, and did not expect them to be sold to anyone?"

Holmes wrote "2) Something hidden in boots" on the blackboard.

Now Lestrade was starting to enjoy the game. "Maybe Selwyn has been lying from the start and his boots were stolen.

Suddenly, the man from whom they were stolen saw him walking down the street, and became so furious that he acted impulsively."

Holmes frowned and nodded, as if he was struggling to take these suggestions seriously. He wrote "3) Boots stolen".

"The simplest possibility," I said, "would probably be that they were stolen by some vagrant or tramp, who had lost his own boots and was desperate for new ones. The weather has been particularly wet and cold these past few days. A homeless man who has no boots might be capable of the rashest of acts."

"That is not a bad conjecture, Doctor," said Lestrade. "Perhaps I should have all the common lodging houses of the vicinity searched?"

Holmes wrote "4) Vagrant" on the board, then took a step back and looked at the list. "Gentlemen, we seem to be taking one step forward and two steps back. The minute a possibility presents itself it is so easily flawed upon closer inspection. Look at this. Number three can be excluded at once, for instance. Unless they were extremely unusual boots of a glaring pastel colour, the previous owner could not possibly have identified them as his old boots in the darkness that night. Number one, well, Watson has time and again reminded me never to underestimate the rage of a wronged husband, but surely Selwyn would not report the theft if he himself was a thief. And if the clothes seller was the thief, then there is no need to direct rage at poor innocent Selwyn. Number four is an attractive proposition, but I deem it as highly unlikely all the same. Any tramp knows full well that if he is in desperate need of a pair of boots, he can get them for free from the nearest charity, or from fellow tramps. Boots are not such a rarity in this metropolis of ours that a tramp – already living on the margins of legality – should wish to incriminate himself in such a thoughtless way." Holmes had drawn a line through all the alternatives as he discarded them, until only one remained. He pondered it for a while. "This eventuality, gentlemen, is highly improbable, but it is the only one that explains why the culprit would carry out the deed in such a sudden and mysterious way. But who would go to the trouble of hiding something precious in something that was up for sale?"

"Maybe he had no time to think up a good hiding place?" suggested Lestrade. "Maybe he was pursued?"

"There are too many maybes and perhaps in this case," complained Holmes. "It's what comes from trying to solve a problem without leaving one's sitting room. Lestrade, do you think we can find out the location of the shop where Selwyn purchased the boots?"

Lestrade smiled a cunning smile and picked up his notebook. "As a matter of fact, I have the address right here."

He had managed to get Holmes just where he had wanted him, and Holmes took the bait. Within minutes, we were in a hansom rattling towards Hackney, and Holmes, ever the machine that only waited for someone to pull his switch, was giddy and ebullient, talking without pause about his recent studies into Elizabethan court proceedings while Lestrade looked increasingly perplexed at the morass of information being heaped upon him.

Finally, we arrived at the little second-hand clothes shop, which was located down a narrow street only accessible by foot. The purveyor was an old Jewish gentleman by the name of Klum, with a crooked back and trouble keeping his skull-cap on his head due to considerable baldness. He approached us just as we entered the cramped and crowded interior of the shop, where rows of rotting old clothes were hanging from the ceiling and across the walls, and were even lying in piles on tables and the floor. Lestrade asked him if he remembered a gentleman who had come a few weeks ago to buy a pair of boots, but Mr Klum only shook his head and said that he had many customers, which was hard to believe from the out-of-the-way location and the general inhospitability of the interior. Holmes asked him where he kept his boots, and the man took us further into the shop to a little room where piles of old shoes were lying on shelves along the walls. A majority of them were sturdy boots of the regular, hard-wearing type preferred by labourers, and although there were varieties in the details, I found it difficult to tell one pair from another, and I assumed that many customers probably walked away from there with an odd pair, judging from the messy way in which they were scattered on the shelves. Holmes picked up a few of them and let his fingers run along the soles and the laces. Then he turned to the proprietor.

"Mr Klum, do you keep any records of who you purchase your items from?"

The man laughed so much that he gave himself a violent cough. "They come to my shop and show me what they have to offer. Sometimes I take it, sometimes I don't."

"But surely," said Lestrade, "you must give them a receipt."

The man only shrugged his shoulders, quite indifferent to Lestrade's authority. The inspector was infuriated by his attitude, but just as he was about to give Mr Klum a lecture in legal matters, Holmes placed his hand on his arm and signalled to us that it was time to leave. Once we were out in the street again, Lestrade and I started to walk down towards the end, only to notice after a few paces that Holmes had stopped in front of the shop and was studying the exterior of the house.

"Have you forgotten something?" asked Lestrade.

Holmes turned to us with a broad smile on his lips. "I thought I had, but I couldn't have, could I?"

He quickly led the way to the nearest thoroughfare and called for a cab. "We have been following the wrong lead," he said. "Our next port of call must be Mr Montague Selwyn."

"In that case," responded Lestrade, "you hardly need a cab. He lives only two streets from here."

"What makes you discard the old clothes shop as a lead?" I asked Holmes as we started walking.

"Because I cannot piece together a likely hypothesis based on the assumption that someone was after the boots that Selwyn purchased. My last theory was that somebody had dropped something into one of the boots from the room lying above the shop. There were wide gaps in the ceiling of the room where Mr Klum kept his shoes, and anybody standing in the room above could easily have dropped something so that it landed in one of the shoes. But as we stepped out, I saw that the upstairs room is empty and has been for quite some time."

"But if the shop cannot tell us anything," said Lestrade, "I fail to see how Mr Selwyn could. He knows nothing of what is going on."

"I suspect that perhaps he knows more than he is aware of," replied Holmes cryptically.

Montague Selwyn's residence was located on the top floor of a terraced house in a street of relative respectability in this otherwise squalid corner of London. We were let in by Selwyn's landlord, a tall and lean gentleman with a large bushy beard whom I was surprised to hear present himself as Dr Wilfred Graves. Hearing that I too was a medical man, he appeared delighted, and pressed my hand with glee, asking whether we would like to come in and have a look at his collection of phrenological specimens. We excused ourselves by repeating the reason for our visit, and Dr Graves informed us that Mr Selwyn had just returned home from his work. His door was only reached by a steep and narrow staircase, and by the time we came to the top, the three of us were all out of breath.

Selwyn looked hesitant when he opened the door, but after Lestrade had explained our business, he was pleased at being treated with such an extensive investigation, and promptly let us in. His home consisted of a small sitting room and what appeared to be an adjoining bedroom, and Mr Selwyn, although obviously unattached, had made the best of his lot by hanging attractive curtains and framed pictures along the walls. Holmes stepped straight in and started to remove his hat and coat, hanging them on a peg by the door. We concluded from this that Holmes intended to interview Selwyn for quite some time, and so we followed his example. Selwyn invited us to sit around the square table that was placed in the centre of the room, but Holmes, to our surprise, declined the offer by explaining that we would not detain him very long.

"There is really only one point in this whole affair that is unclear to me, Mr Selwyn."

"Oh yes? And what might that be?"

Holmes fell silent and looked Mr Selwyn in the eyes.

Selwyn nervously glanced at Lestrade and me. "Did you want to ask me something, sir?"

"I did," said Holmes. "Waking up after that blow on the head, how did you feel?"

"How did I feel?"

"Yes, how did you feel?"

"Well, under the circumstances, I felt alright. I was a bit groggy of course, after the blow, but then when I became aware that my boots were gone, I sort of sobered up."

"I see. Will you please describe exactly what you did upon waking up?"

Selwyn appeared bewildered by these seemingly random queries, but endeavoured to answer as fully as possible. "I sat up, touched my forehead, blinked a few times, got on my legs, walked over to where my cap was lying, picked it up and put it back on my head. It wasn't until then that I noticed my bare feet, and all I could do was walk away in my socks."

"Excellent! Thank you very much, Mr Selwyn, you have been most helpful."

And with these words, Holmes turned to the door and started to put on his coat again. Buttoning it, Holmes looked back at Selwyn with a smile while reaching with one hand towards the bowler that he had hung on a peg. However, he mistakenly grabbed Selwyn's cloth cap that was hanging just beside it and placed it on his head. Realising his mistake, he apologised to Selwyn, laughed awkwardly, and took his bowler.

"Well that was a very rewarding visit, was it not?" said Lestrade sarcastically when we were out on the street.

"Extremely," said Holmes quite seriously.

"Oh, really? Well, we hardly learned anything at all, did we? Apart from the fact that Mr Selwyn felt groggy after being hit on the head, and that he stood up after he had fallen."

"Most instructive, don't you think, Inspector?"

"Please, Mr Holmes, I can take no further from you. And I would appreciate it if in the future you would refrain from taking advantage of my position by pestering innocent crime victims and attempting to steal their hats!"

"Lestrade, please forgive me for applying such unorthodox methods now and then, but I assure you, they are quite effective. I have all the information I need. Now, only a quick examination of the scene of the crime remains."

"Well, then you can do it on your own. I have better things to do."

"Will you direct us there before you go?"

Lestrade sighed impatiently. "Turn right and right again. There is a foul word written on the wall at the entrance of the passage. That should lead you in the right direction."

"Thank you, Lestrade. If you will come around to Baker Street tomorrow afternoon around three o'clock along with some of your men, I will hand over the man who stole Mr Selwyn's boots."

"Are you pulling my leg, Mr Holmes?"

"I am being perfectly serious."

"And why will I need to bring reinforcement?"

"I have reason to believe that this man will not come quietly."

Lestrade snorted, turned his heels and hurried off. Holmes started laughing as soon as he had rounded the corner.

"Holmes," I said, "I am as much in the dark as Lestrade. You have evidently learned something, but I fail to see what it is."

"That is nothing to be ashamed of, my dear Watson. Mr Selwyn does not see either, and he is the victim."

Holmes remained secretive until the following afternoon, being out on errands the entire morning, only to return in time for a late luncheon. He was carrying a large carpet bag with him, which he placed by his armchair before settling himself by the table. I had already eaten by then, and watched him while he devoured his cold leftovers with the appetite of a Bengal tiger. Not for a minute did he look up or acknowledge my presence, and it was not until he put down his knife and fork and joined me by the fire that he showed a readiness to divulge his information.

"Well?" I said, putting aside my book and leaning forward.

"Well what?"

"What have you been up to? Have you cracked the case of the stolen boots?"

"Watson, I have been an utter fool for not realising the truth behind this charade."

"Charade?"

"A cruel charade, no doubt. The crime behind the crime is immoral and hideous, and in a way you were right in ascribing it all to the work of a madman."

"I was? Well, it had to be, hadn't it?"

"Yes. But little did we realise that it was one of the most dangerous and notorious madmen of the country."

"You interest me. Go on."

"It would be foolish to reveal too much before his arrival. After all, not until then can we be absolutely certain of his guilt."

"Arrival? You mean he is coming here?"

"That is what I told Lestrade, is it not? Let's just hope he takes the bait."

"Holmes, your secrecy is insufferable! What on earth could the simple theft of a pair of boots portend other than petty larceny?"

"Watson, you are staring yourself blind at the boots! Forget about the boots, man."

"Forget about the boots? This is not what you would have advised in the Napoleon bust case."

"This is something entirely different. But of course, to focus on the boots is exactly what the culprit wanted us to do.

And I admit that I fell for it to begin with. You see, the clubbing down of an innocent man and the removal of his boots was so strange a crime that it was difficult to see beyond and think that there was something beneath it."

"You mean to say it was some sort of decoy?"

"Precisely."

"From what?"

"Ask yourself, Watson, what do you want to distract someone from by drawing attention to his boots?"

I had no answer to this question, and I was given no time to think about it, for just then the doorbell sounded and a man was let in. We listened to his footsteps as he climbed the stairs to our room. I looked inquiringly at Holmes, but he avoided my gaze and smiled at the door when it was opened. I was completely startled by the unexpected sight of Dr Wilfred Graves, Mr Selwyn's landlord, in the doorframe.

"Ah, Dr Graves," said Holmes. "Do come in."

"I got your note, Mr Burnley," said Graves. "I came as soon as I could." He halted on his way towards the hearthrug. "But you are the gentlemen from yesterday, are you not? Montague Selwyn's friends?"

"Quite so, Dr Graves. Or should I say: Dr Alcott?"

The man's features froze suddenly in a perplexed and enraged grin. I quickly rose from my chair.

"Dr Roderick Alcott?" I exclaimed.

The name was known to me, as indeed it was to any Englishman at that time. It had only been a year since his name was in the papers in connection with the deaths of a number of pregnant women as a result of the misconduct of an established Harley Street practitioner. What had at first seemed like only the example of an inept doctor eventually turned out to be the premeditated doings of a twisted and scheming mind, seemingly intent on using his patients as guinea-pigs in what were unscientific and diseased experiments. Dr Alcott had managed to disappear from view before the police had been able to get their hands on him, however, and since then nobody had managed to trace his whereabouts.

"You are right, Mr Burnley," said our visitor. "I am indeed Roderick Alcott. Or at least I was. I suspected that there was something untoward about your summons, but I could not at first put my finger on it. Now I know what it was. The address. This is not the address of a Mr Patrick Burnley who is interested in selling me some phrenological specimens. This is the address of Sherlock Holmes."

"I am afraid the false name was a necessary precaution, but I did not think you knew about me since you did not seem to recognise us when we visited you yesterday."

"Since my brush with the legal authorities last year I have learned to know where I have my enemies." He drew a short-bladed scalpel from his inside pocket. "And I prefer to keep them at arm's length."

He smiled, and took a quick, stealthy step forward. Holmes remained seated, but I grabbed the poker from the fireplace, the nearest weapon at hand.

"Be calm, Watson," said Holmes. "I have an even more effective weapon."

He produced from the pocket of his dressing-gown a small police whistle, which he raised to his lips. Upon the sharp signal, the door behind Dr Alcott flung open once more, and through it rushed two uniformed policemen followed by Inspector Lestrade. It all happened so quickly that our visitor found no time to react, and the constables had grabbed and handcuffed him before he had been able to swing his blade.

131

"Well, Mr Holmes," said Lestrade. "This is a pretty bird you have caught for us."

"Please, Inspector. I only set the trap. The catching business I leave to your capable hands."

"You scoundrels!" cried Dr Alcott, his eyes wild with agitation.

"Take him outside," instructed Lestrade, and the two husky bobbies pulled him out of the room with little difficulty.

"Well, well, well," said Lestrade. "Little did I suspect when we parted company yesterday that I would lay my hands on Roderick Alcott on my next visit to Baker Street. Climbing the stairs outside, I could hear that he was threatening you, and when I heard his name mentioned, I put two and two together and brought my men up with me."

"Your conduct was impeccable, Inspector," commended Holmes. "I must admit that I had not anticipated that he would be quite so hostile, but it seems he has become rougher in his ways since his fall from grace."

"But what I still do not understand," said I, "is what all this has to do with Montague Selwyn's boots."

"Take your seats by the fire, gentlemen, and all will be explained to you. There. Now, I was also very much in the dark about this case until we arrived at Mr Selwyn's house last night. I was beginning to suspect that this did not really have anything to do with the boots themselves, and when we met Selwyn I started to form a theory in my head. I immediately noticed something curious about Selwyn. He had a small but discernible puncture wound at the back of his head, just behind his right ear. Perhaps I was unconsciously paying attention to his head after Dr Graves had spoken about his phrenological specimens. The wound was of just the type that a thin biopsy needle leaves behind. Therefore, it seemed to me relevant to ask Selwyn firstly how he felt after waking up from the assault, and secondly to ascertain whether he still had his hat on his head when he woke up. By detailing his movements upon waking up, he revealed to me that his cap had been lying quite a distance from where he had been lying, as he had to get up and walk over to it. As I had removed my hat and coat, I was able to pretend to take the wrong hat upon leaving, which allowed me to inspect Selwyn's cap up close. There were small splotches of dried blood at the place where his puncture wound would have rubbed against the lining of the cap.

"It all seemed perfectly clear to me. What better and more simple way of distracting someone whose head you have just been meddling with, than to remove his boots seemingly without reason, so that all his thoughts go to his feet rather than his head. Hitting him on the head of course also disguises the possible pain left by the incision."

"So you mean," said I, "that Dr Alcott used Mr Selwyn for an experiment in phrenology, piercing a thin part of his skull with a biopsy needle?"

"Naturally. This was his current obsession, as he himself unwittingly told us. I have spent the morning doing some research into the field, and I have found that there is currently a scholarly discussion going on about the possible effects on a man's mind from piercing the skull in this way. One of the most fervent article writers is Dr Wilfred Graves. I also made some investigations on the house that Dr Graves lives in, and found that it was purchased a little over a year ago by a cousin of Dr Roderick Alcott."

"By Jove!" cried Lestrade. "This is excellent work, Mr Holmes. So simple, and yet so momentous."

"It was really only about making a certain connection, and then all the other pieces of the puzzle fell into place. On our way from the clothes shop, I asked myself, what if the removal of the boots was just meant as a distraction, what would it be a distraction from? When Dr Graves mentioned phrenology, that was it. The best way to distract from the head is to draw attention to the feet!"

"Marvellous." Lestrade was almost jumping up and down. "Simply marvellous."

"Oh, by the way," said Holmes. "I also revisited the scene of the crime this morning, and when I walked around the area I found these flung into a rubbish bin." He opened the large carpet bag that had been standing next to his armchair and produced a pair of worn and dirty hobnailed boots. "Perhaps Mr Selwyn would like them back as a souvenir of his adventure?"

The Remarkable Experience of Professor Parkins

The case which I am about to recount reached the public shortly after its occurrence in a form that omitted certain aspects crucial to its solution. The involvement of my friend Mr Sherlock Holmes in the investigation of it was never reported, nor was the fact that it was satisfyingly solved, thus turning the story into a famous case of an unexplained haunting rather than a psychologically interesting study of mental manipulation. I put forth this version not to defame Prof. M. R. James, nor to suggest that his account was flawed by sensationalism, but as a tribute to his excellent narrative skills, and maybe my version will only serve to make commonplace that which he made captivating.

It was the beginning of January, in the very first days of the new year, when, it seems, the world has completely forgotten that only a brief moment ago it was consumed by a festive holiday spirit, and the dull featureless existence of a long winter commences. I had been celebrating the holidays with relatives in the country, but when I returned to London, I was reminded of Holmes, and decided to pay him a long overdue visit in hope of cheering him up. I had been foolish, of course, in thinking that he would be depressed at the prospect of spending Christmas by himself. Holmes was never depressed by anything other than a lack of work, and when I stepped into our old sitting-room at Baker Street, the thick atmosphere of shag tobacco that met me was a clear indication that he might well have been shut up in this room since mid-December.

At the sound of the door, he peered up from behind the back of his armchair, and welcomed me heartily.

"Watson! Such a pleasure. I dare say you will be staying for lunch?"

"If you wish me to," I said and walked up to my old place next to him. "I trust you have had a pleasant Christmas?"

"Hmm?" Holmes was distracted by some papers that had been laying in his lap, and which he was now carelessly pushing down on the floor. "Has Christmas been? I must admit, dear fellow, that it has passed me quite by. I have been absorbed by a most engaging study into a couple of fascinating incunabula that I managed to retrieve from a bookshop in Charing Cross Road."

"As a result of which you simply happened to miss Christmas and New Year's Eve?"

"That too? Well, if only a case had come my way, I would at least have found an excuse to leave the house, but people have become so excruciatingly law-abiding these days."

"Holmes, if I didn't know you better, I would think you would commit a crime yourself one of these days if only to have something to solve."

"That would require me to forget how I had gone about it immediately after I had committed the crime. Hm! Which would make it very nearly the perfect crime! A somnambulist, perhaps, quite unaware of his own wrong-doing."

"Or maybe you could commit it to fiction, like so many people nowadays."

"Fiction? Ha! Don't you think the world is big enough as it is? But soft, as Shakespeare would say, unless I am mistaken that was the sound of the doorbell."

And sure enough, within moments heavy steps were heard ascending the stairs, and a gentleman stood in the doorframe. He was a large, heavyset fellow, balding, though barely middle-aged, and with a pair of very small wire-rimmed

136

spectacles on his nose. His get-up was slightly dishevelled, but in a way that suggested a lack of routine rather than a breach of it. Holmes stood up and greeted him, introducing ourselves.

"Good day, gentlemen," said our visitor. "My name is Perivale Parkins, professor of ontography at Cambridge. I apologise for coming to you unannounced, but I have a matter I would like to have your opinion on, unless you are otherwise engaged?"

"Please, take a seat, Professor, and lay your problem before us. We shall help you in any way we can."

The man took a seat, showing some signs of impatience, while Holmes eyed him discreetly.

"I understand, Mr Holmes," he began, "that you are a man of reason?"

"I hope so."

"And you would not accept uncritically a statement professing to be an account of the supernatural?"

Holmes glanced at me. "On seven occasions, Watson and I have been called out to investigate phenomena purporting to be proof of the supernatural. In all cases, we have been able to show that they were examples of the incredible or the grotesque, but never the supernatural. The curious thing is, Professor, that people assume that the supernatural is the paragon of the strange and amazing, when my experience tells me that often that place should be assigned to the strange and disgusting freaks of human nature."

"Your attitude is reassuring. I am in considerable need of reassurance in this matter. You see, until a few weeks ago, I was the most stern opposer of the supernatural, or indeed of magic or religion, or any thing beyond that which is verifiable according to the laws of science. I am known among my colleagues and friends for my unwillingness to concede to claims of the paranormal."

"And then something happened to make you waver?" I conjectured.

"Quite so. It was the end of full term, and I was planning on spending a few days in the country before Christmas. I have just taken up golf, you see, and was eager to devote myself to it as much as I could before the obligations of the holidays. A friend of mine had recommended the little town of Burnstow on the east coast, and I booked myself into a hotel called the Globe Inn, which was the only place not shut up at this time of the year. An archaeologist friend mentioned to me before leaving that Burnstow was the site of an old preceptory of the Knights Templar, and suggested I have a look at it to see if it would be suitable for excavation. I was only too glad to oblige him, and promised that I would write to him with details of the lay of the land.

"The Globe was a fine enough hotel, but since it was the only place open in the area, I had to make do with their last room, which had two beds in it and a dodgy gas radiator. As for the rest of the place it was rather dull, and the other boarders were golfers, like me. I conversed with a few of them at dinner, and was utterly bored in the process. Only one of them seemed to share my interests and promise conversation at a slightly superior level compared to the others. His name was Wilson, a retired colonel up from London seeking to improve his handicap. He invited me to join him for a brandy on that first evening, and he was interested to hear about my research. We spoke for about half an hour on diverse topics, including politics, art and philosophy. Eventually, however, it transpired that the man was devoutly religious, and when I implied in what I told him about my work that I was a sceptic, he started to become uneasy. I managed to steer clear of the most flagrant discord, and although the man was clearly put off by what I said, we decided we would join each other for a round of golf the next day.

"I dare say the old army man was approaching the day when he would be forced to give up the game, for only an hour after teeing off, he started looking pale and worn. We finished the game in due course, but it seemed that the colonel's debility influenced his comportment. He became increasingly irritated and snappy, and I struggled during the last hour to maintain the civilised level of conduct in which we had begun. I suggested he return to the hotel for a cup of tea before dinner, which he said he would do. As for myself, I had remembered the promise I gave to my archaeologist colleague, and fancied I would walk back along the beach to try and find the remnants of that preceptory he had been talking about. I thought it was a good excuse to avoid the company of Colonel Wilson for a while.

"I found my way from the golf course down to the shingle beach, and came upon a narrow path that led through the undergrowth bordering onto it. It was growing dark quite quickly now, and I hurried along for fear of losing my way. As I did so, my foot must have got caught in a root or something, because all of a sudden I fell forwards and tumbled a good way down a grassy slope. When I got my bearings, I noticed I was surrounded by a selection of low mounds. I examined the area, and came to the conclusion that this was the very place I had been looking for. The mounds consisted of blocks of flint put together with mortar and overgrown with grass and bramble. I was delighted at my discovery, and glad to be able to bring my friend the good news. This would be an easy place to excavate, and easier still for me to estimate the layout of it. I paced the site and managed to get an idea of the buildings and their scale. In the centre, the mounds were arranged in a circle, suggesting the type of round church the Templars were in the habit of constructing, and there was still light enough for me to sketch out a plan of the place in my notebook.

"I was just about to leave, satisfied with the work I had done, when I made an amazing discovery. At the end of the site, I found a large flat stone. At first I thought it must be some sort of monolith that had fallen over, but upon closer examination, it seemed to me rather that it had been placed like that to form some sort of altar. I stepped up on top of it and let my hand slide across the surface. At one end, there was a break in the stone, suggesting a cavity. I produced my penknife, and poked into the hole. I tried to light it up with a match, but the sea wind kept blowing the flame out. Tapping into the bottom of the cavity, I could feel something moving about down there. I reached my hand down, and picked it up. There was barely light to see, but I reckoned it was man-made, a metal stick, about four inches long. Deciding I would examine it later, I let it slip into my pocket, and within seconds I was on my way.

"To make sure I would find my way back to the Globe in the twilight, I chose the easy way of walking on the beach. After a minute or two, I looked back to see if the ruins were visible from the beach, when I saw that there was somebody behind me. A dark figure was moving on the beach in the same direction as me. I didn't think much about it at first, but after looking over my shoulder a few more times, I fancied that the figure, although clearly moving, was not getting any closer to me, and all the time, it was far enough from me to make identifying it impossible. It was just a silhouette. The experience – I will not deny it – upset me, and I walked faster.

By the time I turned inland to walk the last yards up to the hotel, the figure was still there. I must admit I ran the last bit.

"I do not know why I was seized by such apprehension then on the beach. I suppose we all have the instinct for fear whenever we are confronted by something strange, and I do believe that the fear of darkness is something that we are born with rather than a fear of what may lurk within that darkness. But the rest of my story destabilises my attempts at rationalisation.

"First there was the object I found at the preceptory. I had quite forgotten about it until the boy at the hotel informed me it had fallen out of my pocket while he had been brushing my coat. After an evening of bridge with the colonel, I retired to my room and sat down to inspect it. I was startled to find that it was made of bronze, and a few minutes of scratching away cakes of mud off the surface informed me that it was a pipe rather than a stick, and more than a pipe, it was a whistle! It was exquisitely made, and very attractive, and what's more it looked quite ancient. Holding it up to the light, I saw to my astonishment that the carvings on it which I had taken for a primitive pattern, were actually writing. In due course, I had deciphered the print and copied it out in my notebook."

The professor produced a small notebook from his pocket and read from it: "'Fla fur bis fle.' That was one side. And on the other side there was: 'Quis est iste qui venit.'"

I noticed how Holmes worded the two sentences quietly to himself, discreetly committing them to memory.

"My knowledge of Latin is sizable enough," continued the professor, "for me to be able to translate the latter one. 'Who is this who is coming?' I suppose would be the closest rendition. The other one eludes me. I interpreted the phrase as referring to the one who would come in answer to the whistle. I was now

141

so animated by my discovery that I simply put it to my lips and blew it. The sound was quite astonishing, both beautiful and mysterious. I was interrupted in my work by a sudden violent gust of wind that managed to force open the windows, and it took me quite some time to close them again. In the silence that followed, I could hear the colonel pacing in his room above me; I had apparently woken him. This business quite distracted me from my examination of the whistle, and I decided to go to bed. A sleepless night ensued, characterised only by an occasional dream of the beach I had walked on that afternoon, and the black figure on it.

"Please don't think me weak-minded, gentlemen, but I was sure at some moments during that night that I could hear something stirring in the dark corners of my room. It can of course be ascribed to rats, the faulty gas fixtures or whatnot, but the next morning, as I was preparing for another round with the colonel, the maid came into my room with an extra blanket for the bed. She stopped halfway towards it, however, and asked me on what bed she should put it. When I asked the girl what she meant, she said that she had made both of them up that morning, as it seemed both of them had been slept in. In the dim morning light, I had not noticed this, and it seemed very strange to me, although I could not help but think of the sounds I had heard that night. Nevertheless, I banished all these thoughts from my mind, and spent the day on the golf course. This second game was much more enjoyable than the first, but as we walked back to the club house afterwards, our conversation happened to venture into the area of folklore, when the colonel remarked on the wind last night and how he had heard someone whistling, which reminded him of the common superstition of it being able to create a wind by whistling for it.

"An argument was again avoided, however, since a boy ran up to us, looking very out of breath and a little frightened. He told us he had seen something in one of the windows of the Globe while he had been watering plants with the garden hose in the front lawn. It was a figure standing in the window, all white, waving at him. I believed he was talking a lot of nonsense, and said so, but the colonel insisted we go back to investigate, so we did. There was no one in the windows when we came to the hotel, but the window that fit the description the boy had given could only be my own window, which made me laugh. I said there could not possibly be anyone in my room, since I had taken care to lock it when I left that morning. All the same, we went up, finding the door still locked, and I remarked to the colonel that I didn't like it when servants went in and out of rooms that should be locked. Stepping into the room, the colonel drew my attention to one of the beds, in which the sheets had been upset. I told him this was not the bed I was using, and that clearly a crime had been committed. Nothing seemed to have been stolen, however, and the maid, when questioned, said she had made the beds that morning, and that neither she nor anyone else had been in the room after that.

"Since the staff at the hotel all seemed to me to be decent people, my suspicions fell on the boy who had given us the news. I concluded that he must have been lying, and that we had fallen victim to his childish prank. The colonel did not seem to agree with my supposition, but said nothing, and we left it there. There was no further conversation between us that evening, and dinner passed in silence. It wasn't until we went up to our beds that I was reminded of my whistle. I had made some passing mention of it to the colonel, and wanted to show it to him, thinking he might make something out of the inscription. He looked at it closely, and there was immediately something anxious about his face. I told him I might hand it over to an archaeologist at Cambridge, or maybe present it to a museum, but he only frowned and told me I'd be better off chucking it into the sea. I don't know what made him say this, but by now I had really had enough of him, and bade him goodnight.

"That night, I experienced the most fantastic and fearful occurrence of my life. Once more, I was tossing and turning in my bed, and it was not until I rose to draw the curtains that I noticed to my great surprise that they were gone. In fact, the entire curtain rod had been removed. I assumed it was the maid who had done it to wash the curtains and then forgotten to replace them, and since it was late I did not want to make a fuss, so I managed to make up for it by making use of my railway rug. In the middle of the night, however, I was woken by the sound of my rug falling from its place, leaving the window bare. The moon shone brightly into the room, and I wondered whether I should go to the trouble of rearranging it. Just then, I heard the sound that had disturbed me the previous night. It was the sound of someone, or something, shifting in the other bed. Within seconds, I was out of my bed, grasping my walking stick, when I saw, as clearly as I see you now, a figure rising up from beneath the sheets, and sitting upright in the bed. And then, suddenly, it bolted up, and stood on the floor, right in between the two beds. It now blocked the door and started to float through the room towards me. It was a figure, much the size of a man, a tall man, but if you were to ask me to describe it, I could only say that it was all bed linen.

"I backed towards the window, which by now was my only escape. It came closer, and I could not keep myself from crying out. Upon hearing this, it was as if it had finally managed to locate me, for now it hurried towards me, and was only inches from me, when the door was thrust open and Colonel Wilson appeared, framed by the light from the corridor outside. And with his appearance, it was as if the creature vanished into thin air, or at least whatever it had been which had filled the sheets, for they were still there, but simply fell onto the floor in a large jumble. The colonel came up to me, and managed to calm me down. I dropped onto my bed, and I must have fallen asleep, or fainted. When I woke up, it was daylight, and I saw that the colonel had slept in the other bed, wrapped in a rug. The linen was still on the floor by the window.

"He and I had a long talk after breakfast, during which we tried to wrap our heads around what had happened, and what we had both seen, for he maintained that he had also seen the figure, just before it disappeared. I am afraid that I found it impossible to hold onto my rationalist outlook in this intercourse, and the colonel was most understanding. I gave him the whistle to dispose of, and he threw it into the sea, just as he had advised me to do. The next day we both left the Globe, and I returned to Cambridge, only to find that I could not leave this whole experience behind me. I spent all of Christmas trying to occupy my mind with other things, but it kept haunting me, not least because I simply cannot incorporate it into my worldview. And so, last night, I decided that I would put the matter into your hands. Perhaps it is too late to investigate it, but simply telling you about my experience will put me at ease, knowing that another rational mind will have the opportunity to meditate on it."

The professor fell silent, removing his spectacles to polish them with his handkerchief. Holmes was tapping his fingertips on the armrests of his chair.

"Have you spoken to your archaeologist friend since you came back?" he asked.

"I have not. I did not feel it was very urgent, and besides, he is away until the beginning of next term."

"And what happened to the bed clothes?"

Parkins lowered his eyes. "Since I was so panic-stricken, I insisted that they were burned, and paid the hotel-owners for a new set."

"Did you or anyone else examine them?"

"No. Wilson carried them from the room and out into the back garden, where the landlord burned them."

"I see. And there was no formal inquiry conducted?"

"Oh no. I could not have faced it, and the hotel-owners indicated that they did not want rumours spread about their house."

"That is understandable," I remarked.

"Yes, but hardly helpful to us," said Holmes. "What else can you tell us about Colonel Wilson?"

"Well, what do you have in mind?"

"His first name?"

"Desmond, I think. He told me he is club secretary at the Burlington Club and I believe he takes rooms in St James's. I also seem to remember him telling me he is a widower, when he explained about his strong religious feelings."

"How did he come across to you when you elaborated on your rationalist standpoint?"

"He was very controlled and took care not to make passionate statements, but it was clear to me he was uncomfortable. So was I. In the end, I think we came to a sort of silent truce which derived from our not approaching the subject again. And, of course, I was more compliant after my nocturnal experience."

146

"Ah yes, that," Holmes remarked, as if the incident was only a marginal aspect of the affair. "Did you ever have the opportunity of inspecting the other bed?"

"Not really. When the maid mentioned that both had been slept in, I was angry with her, and left my room without trying to make heads or tails of it."

"Was it the same type of bed as the one you slept in?"

Parkins raised his hands. "Mr Holmes, I appreciate your interest, but I fear your attempts at comprehending the matter is in vain. I understand that your impulse is to solve the mystery, but I am starting to think it has no natural solution. I only came here to share my experience with you, to unload my burden, as it were, and now that I have done so, I already feel better."

"So the experience has managed to convert you?" I said.

The professor looked my way, and seemed a bit surprised at hearing it so frankly put. "Yes. Maybe it has." His gaze wandered, as if he only now realised the extent of this business.

We were interrupted by Holmes loudly clapping his hands together and bouncing out of his armchair.

"Well then, there is not much more we can do for you. I hope you don't think your visit has been in vain, and I promise you we will get back to you if we should have any further thoughts on the matter."

Parkins looked content and was also on his feet.

"I thank you for your time, gentlemen. You may reach me at this address." He handed Holmes a card and walked towards the door. He stopped on the threshold, hesitated for a second, then turned back to us. "There is just one more thing."

Holmes stepped up to him. "Yes?"

"It is nothing, but I mention it, simply because I cannot fit it into the rest of the story. When I woke up after having fainted, the room was exactly like it had been except for one thing. The curtains were back. Good day to you."

And with these words he left the room. Holmes closed the door behind him and returned to his seat with a smile. After a while, he became aware of my startled look. "Is something the matter, Watson?"

"I just think you could have been a bit more stubborn."

"We did what he asked us to do. We listened to his story."

"But what a story! Don't try to tell me you weren't intrigued by it."

"On the contrary, my dear Watson. I found it very interesting indeed. Not to mention fraught with unexplored aspects which might very well provide the investigator with a natural solution. But you heard the man! His mind was made up. Besides, there was not much more he could tell us."

Holmes started filling his briar.

"But do you intend to investigate it?" I asked.

"Yes and no. On the one hand, there is not much to investigate. It happened several weeks ago, and whatever traces there might have been at the hotel must be obliterated by now. Not to mention deliberately burned. On the other hand, it is intriguing to the point of being quite irresistible. And there is one lead which we may very well follow up."

"Which one?"

"Colonel Desmond Wilson of the Burlington Club."

Holmes lit the pipe and stretched out his legs in front of him.

"Three-pipe?" I inquired.

"Just so. But unless you are otherwise engaged, you may return this evening to see the case through."

I had a few appointments at my practice that afternoon, one of which took much longer than I had expected, and it was well past six o'clock by the time I returned to Baker Street. Stepping through the door of the sitting room, I found it empty, but then suddenly, a white sheet jumped out from behind a window curtain with a booming wail. It only took me a second to realise that it was Holmes playing me a prank, and though I smiled at him, his trick, or perhaps moreso the fact that, for a fraction of a second, I had fallen for it, quite annoyed me.

"Holmes, you rascal," I said, barely hiding my irritation.

He pulled back the sheet, revealing a laughing face. "Please forgive me, my friend, for playing you such a simple trick, but you have also helped me in my work."

"Indeed? How so?"

Holmes carelessly folded up the sheet into a bundle and threw it over the sofa.

"I wanted to know how an average reasonable man, and preferably one of a scientific schooling, would react when faced with an evidently bogus ghost."

"And what is the conclusion of your experiment?"

"A most interesting one. Have a seat and help yourself to the sherry, and I will tell you what progress I have made since this morning."

I did as he advised, and had soon forgotten my recent humiliation.

"It is remarkable, is it not," began Holmes, "how most of us, in spite of our living in a modern age of reason, instinctively react to sights we cannot instantly explain as if they were encounters with the supernatural. You tried very well to hide your unease when confronted with my ghost, but I must say that even through the little holes I had cut into the sheet with a pair of scissors your instant reaction was apparent in your face. You did believe, if only for a very brief moment, that I was a ghost."

I shifted in my seat at the hearing of this, but saw no point in vainly contradicting him.

"You need not be ashamed of this, Watson. I think any man would react in the same way. The question is why. There we very nearly move into your territory, old man. I believe that, deeply embedded into our subconscious, are conceptions which we have inherited from our forefathers, conceptions which have been created over a very long time, and a time during which, until only a century ago, most people did believe in the supernatural. And I think these conceptions constitute our natural instincts, the wild men within us expecting to meet goblins and devils while walking in the dark forest."

"It is an interesting theory, Holmes. But it rests on the assumption that everybody is at heart a believer rather than a sceptic."

"Well, to put it another way: we are first and foremost animals with primitive beliefs, and secondly civilised human beings with sophisticated beliefs. The primitive animal is dying within us, because it only took half a second for you to look through my disguise. But the more believable the apparition which confronts us, the more room to thrive we give to the irrationalist within. Thus, when we encounter a thing like that witnessed by Professor Parkins in his hotel room, which resists the most fervent attempts at rationalisation, our power of reason is severely damaged. Even a devout rationalist such as he finds reason to adjust his worldview."

"That sounds reasonable enough," I said. "But it hardly explains what it was he saw."

"On the contrary, Watson. It explains why he reacted as he did to what he saw, and his reaction is the most important aspect of this whole business. About a hundred years ago, an interesting case took place in Hammersmith. You may have heard stories of the Hammersmith Ghost?"

"Yes, I'm sure I have. Several witnesses in the area claiming to have seen a white-clad apparition wandering the streets at night."

"Exactly. It even came to the point where a local armed patrol was formed, and the leader of it shot dead a poor innocent plasterer on his way home, simply because the man was wearing the customary white clothes of his trade. The murderer, though, was eventually aquitted, since the jury thought he had been acting under the influence of the current state of panic following the ghost sightings. Consequently, all of a sudden shooting a man in cold blood was no longer a hanging matter."

"I see your point. The reactions to the sightings created the hysteria that resulted in both a murder and the aquittal of the murderer."

"And what was the cause of it? Eventually a local shoemaker stepped forward, admitting he had been dressing up in a sheet to get even on his apprentice, who had been scaring the shoemaker's children with ghost stories."

"You should be thankful I did not draw a gun at you!"

"You see, Watson? This business was the consequence of a man dressing up in no better way than I just did. Can you imagine the result if someone tried a little harder to trick a man?"

"So you don't think what Professor Parkins saw was a ghost?"

"Don't be ridiculous, Watson. Ghosts don't haunt second-rate hotel rooms. I can think of a lot of better things I would do if I were dead."

"Well, how do you explain it then?"

"I have been sitting here by myself all day. I am tired of my own thoughts. What are your reflections?"

I sipped my glass of sherry, trying to come up with some concrete hypotheses. "I cannot say I have been wracking my brains on this problem all day, like you. But it does seem to me that the most apparent theory would be to assume that there was another person in Parkins' room."

"I quite agree, Watson, but how do you account for this person's sudden disappearance right in front of Parkins' eyes?"

"It was the middle of the night and he had been sleeping. Perhaps he wasn't quite awake yet? Or perhaps he was fast asleep still, all of it simply being a really violent nightmare?"

"Ah, you mean it was a nightmare as in the old definition of the word? The incubus riding its victim. Demons creeping out of their hiding places by the shelter of darkness."

"Well, not exactly, old fellow, do try to take me a bit seriously. I am trying to give you as good natural explanations as I can come up with. For instance, I know some doctors who have ascribed nightmares and ghost sightings to indigestion."

Holmes bobbed in his seat. "Was it not how Ebenezer Scrooge accounted for his experiences? 'An undigested bit of beef, a blot of mustard, a crumb of cheese, a fragment of an underdone potato.' Well, these are all perfectly decent explanations for strange phenomena, but they don't quite fit this particular case, do they?"

"You could relieve me of my agony by just saying what conclusion you have reached yourself."

"I have reached none as yet. But I have been staring myself blind at the strange details of the case, for I believe they hold the key to the solution."

"Such as?"

"Such as the curious disappearance and reappearance of the curtains in Professor Parkins' hotel room."

"There is no mystery about that. The maid removed them to be cleaned and only replaced them in the morning."

"Yes, perhaps."

"What else?"

"Well, that is really it, apart from the more apparent things, like the little boy and the figure he saw in the window, and the immediate destruction of the bed clothes, all of which point to the inference that Colonel Wilson is behind it all somehow."

"Aren't you forgetting something?"

"What?"

"The tin whistle that Parkins found."

"What about it?"

"It just seems that it plays some part in this. Professor Parkins implicitly connects it to the ghost, and his narrative was founded on the notion that his playing it summoned something from the other side."

"The only thing it summoned, Watson, was a devilish plan of deception. I'm tired of sitting in this chair now, it is time to act. Get your hat and coat and we will be on our way."

"Where to?"

"The Burlington Club!"

Holmes was visibly annoyed during our cab ride to St James's, mumbling to himself and impatiently knocking on the windowsill with his knuckles. Holmes had insisted on a growler instead of a hansom, but the noise from the traffic outside was still too loud for me to be able to hear what he was whispering to himself, although at one point it seemed to me he was repeating one word over and over. "How? How? How?" I made some feeble attempts at reassuring him, quoting his own motto about eliminating the impossible until the only likely scenario remains.

"That is what you have done," I said.

"Yes, but I still have no answer. I know what did not happen, but I do not know what did happen."

"Then we shall ask him."

"Ask him?"

"Exactly. We are quite certain he has something to do with it, are we not? Then we will ask him how it was done."

"I don't know, Watson."

"Come, Holmes. This despondency is not like you."

"It has been increasing of late. Oh Watson, it's at times such as these I get images in my head of that farm in the Sussex Downs."

"You have been talking about that farm for years, Holmes, but you never seem to be able to acquire one. You are a town rat, Holmes, you would not last a fortnight living in the countryside."

But he wasn't listening. The driver had stopped at an intersection, and Holmes was looking out the window at the commotion on the pavement. There was an unusually large crowd of people assembled there for some reason. When Holmes turned his head back to me, he was smiling broadly.

"I think we will be able to face our adversary with our heads held up high."

As our cab started moving again, he chuckled and rubbed his hands together, every inch the cunning reasoner I was so familiar with. He had evidently made a mental leap that rekindled his confidence.

"I say, what happened, Holmes?"

"Only something that should have happened several hours ago. I hope I'm not losing my touch, Watson. But I can hardly be blamed, for it is a very clever and devious man we are dealing with. And oh, what a sinister thing it is he has done. What a pleasure it will be to reveal it."

Holmes' epiphany could hardly have come at a better time, for we were now turning into one of the back lanes adjoining Piccadilly, which was the location of the Burlington Club. This club had been completely unknown to me, and its address seemed to guarantee its place in the margins of clubland respectability while at the same time safely ensconced in relative obscurity. Holmes had made some researches into it during the day, uncovering that its origins were of quite recent date, being a branch of a religious organisation which had established some mission chapels in the most spiritually deprived areas of the East End.

"As far as I can apprehend," said Holmes, "it is a sleepy congregation of retired vicars and charitably minded elderly gentlemen of modest means who wish to signify connections with a club that lies in the neighbourhood of the more respectable London clubs. The image, then, is hardly one of a diabolical circle of criminals, which, of course, in itself is exceedingly suspicious."

We came to a halt in front of an unassuming door without steps, wedged in between houses of a more grand appearance. Holmes paid the cab driver while I accosted it. A minuscule brass plaque next to it read "The Burlington. Gentlemen's Social Club." Below it was a bell, which Holmes' gloved hand quickly reached out and pulled.

"What is the plan?" I asked him.

"If my estimation of this man is correct," he replied, "it will be enough to let him know that we know. That, I think, will frighten him sufficiently."

"What do we know?"

Holmes turned to me. "Just agree with everything I say, Watson."

"Right you are, Holmes."

The door was opened by a liveried servant, who let us into a very small front room with only a desk and a man in it. The man rose from his chair behind the desk, saying, quite simply:

"Yes?"

"We are looking for Colonel Desmond Wilson," stated Holmes frankly.

The man asked us to wait, and disappeared through a door at the back. The servant stood to attention next to us, but the diminutive size of the room gave me the feeling he was peering over my shoulder, making it impossible for Holmes and me to talk privately. Thus there were a few moments of silence until the receptionist returned with a distinguished elderly gentleman in tow. His age and his bearing made for an unlikely villain in this drama, but while being scrutinised by his penetrating gaze as we introduced us, I felt that there was shrewdness and duplicity behind his façade.

"What can I do for you, gentlemen?" he asked.

"We are operating on account of Professor Perivale Parkins, whom I believe you are acquainted with," said Holmes.

The man searched his memory. "Parkins, Parkins, ah yes, Parkins. I met him at Burnstow a few weeks ago. Yes, a decent sort of man. Is there any trouble?"

"It concerns the strange event that occurred on his last night there."

"I see." The man looked at us each in turn. "Perhaps it is better that we speak in private. If you would come this way, please."

We were shown into a small and comfortably furnished room, evidently kept for the benefit of non-members. Curiously, it was windowless, and its walls were covered in thick dark hangings, muffling every sound we made while entering.

The colonel invited us to sit in a pair of leather armchairs. "Now then, gentlemen."

"I think you know why we are here," said Holmes.

The colonel smiled benevolently, the picture of innocence. "Do I?"

"Your trick was very well executed, if I may say so, but I am afraid you underestimated the power of reason."

"I'm sure I don't know what you are talking about."

"Then perhaps you will let me give you my version of what took place?"

"If you think it will help."

"Your scheme was cunning indeed, considering it was improvised in a short time and was an adaptation to the situation at hand. Professor Parkins did react on your devout religiosity, since he is a man of science, but it is nothing out of the ordinary, so he would never suspect it to be the motive of a crime. But in fact your plan started to take shape just after that very first conversation after dinner, did it not? At least you must have decided early on that you would prove your point to him in no uncertain terms, and perhaps even convert him in the process. The first thing you did was to follow Professor Parkins after you had parted on the golf course. He went to examine an old ruin, and you looked for an opportunity to scare him, but did not get the chance until he started walking back to the hotel in the fading light. Then you hit upon the idea of making yourself visible on the beach but at such a distance he would not be able to identify you in the gloom. It was a safe plan, for you knew he thought you were resting in your room and would not disturb you when he came back to the hotel.

"In the night, you crept into the professor's room, making sure you were hiding in the shadows all along, and upset the bed clothes in the unused bed. This nocturnal visit also gave you an opportunity to examine the room, upon which you came across the gas radiator. Parkins' sleep was uneasy due to the sight of you on the beach, not to mention the way you banged his window open with your walking stick to make it seem they had been blown open by the wind. As your room was above his, there were a number of things you could do to frighten him. The detail of the old whistle that Parkins had found only served to make your hauntings more eerie.

"You started to enjoy having this man in your power. You bribed a little boy to tell you about the ghost, since you knew that he would only fall for it if was seen by another. You could of course have found a more respectable witness, but he played the part admirably. Everything was set for the finishing touch, the next night. By this time, you had become a bit carried away, but you were enjoying it too much. Besides, it was all in a good cause. Your plan was brilliant because it was so simple. A ghost is invisible and immaterial. It is made of air. Or, in this case, gas. Yes, you really managed to fool Professor Parkins, and when he came to see us, he was quite convinced that he had seen a ghost. But there were points in his story that did not fit in with the way he had interpreted it. And it took me a while to realise how I was going to interpret it. All the time, I knew that the curtains were the key to the mystery, and by removing the curtains in the professor's room, you both bothered the professor and found the last ingredient in your plan. The curtain rod. By connecting it to the sconce that supplied the radiator with gas, you could lead the gas up to the other bed, concealing the rod underneath the bed clothes. You then turned the gas up and quickly left the room. There were no certainties about the plan, anything could happen, but it gave the best possible results. The gas turned the sheet into a hot-air balloon, inflating it, and even making it rise up from the bed, giving the impression of a spectral figure hovering over the floor. When you had heard the professor's screams, making sure the illusion had produced an effect, you bolted into the room and immediately turned down the gas. Luckily, Professor Parkins fainted, which gave you the time to remove the rod from the gas sconce, and put it back in the window. There was no chance the professor would look through this, since his reaction to the ghost had reassured you of its effect. Perhaps seeing his reaction even made you feel that you had gone a bit too far?"

Colonel Wilson's face had changed during Holmes' narrative, from mild complacency into a resolute frown. "What do you want from me?" he said, betraying a slight tremor in his voice.

"Only your confession, Colonel. Perhaps even a note stating as much addressed to Professor Parkins."

"That would only serve to inflate his smugness. He was the archetypal self-righteous scientist, looking down on ordinary churchgoing people. I only wanted to teach him a lesson."

"Your lesson turned him into a broken man. And it seems to have turned you into the archetypal self-righteous churchgoer."

Wilson's gaze flickered. "How did you manage to piece all this together?"

"By noting all the things Professor Parkins told me that he did not attach any importance to. The gas radiator, your room being above his, the curtain rod. It all pointed in one direction. I may have made some guesses, but the reactions in your face when I explained it proved me right. Oh, and, by the way; the whistle."

"What about it?"

"If you will hand it over to me, I will return it to the professor."

I was just as startled as the colonel.

"Are you implying that I am a thief? I threw it into the sea!"

"Stuff and nonsense, Colonel. Your interest in that religious artefact inspired your plan just as much as your will to teach the professor a lesson. You never threw it away."

Holmes held out his hand. The colonel leaned forward in his chair, resting his elbows on his knees. Then he stood up, nodded to us and left the room. In less than a minute he returned, walked round the back of Holmes' chair, paused and handed him something, before walking back to his own seat. Holmes now held in his hand a short, smooth-surfaced metal pipe with a few holes along the side.

"Thank you, Colonel. We will wait while you write that note."

Holmes rose and led the way out of the room. A few minutes later, Colonel Wilson emerged, and handed Holmes an envelope.

"It was never my intention to break the man completely. I was, as you say, carried away by the venture. But I maintain that my mission all along was to smash his scientific pride."

"Just as mine is to smash religious pride," replied Holmes. "Good evening."

It was a relief to come outside into the fresh and crisp air, such a change from the stifled atmosphere of the club. Holmes expressed a wish to walk back, which I readily seconded.

"I cannot think how you ever hit upon the idea of the curtain rod and the gas radiator," I confessed.

"The curiosity of the curtains struck me from the beginning, but I could not fit it into any likely scenario. The rest of the story, I must admit, I put together through pure conjecture, but it was only a matter of deciding upon a natural explanation and that the colonel was the culprit, and all the parts of the story fell into place. There were really no other way of interpreting the events once Parkins' supernatural perspective had been eliminated. But the way he had done it eluded me until the last moment. It wasn't until we were on our way here that it hit me. Do you remember the cab stopped at a crossing, and there was quite a large crowd of people on the pavement?"

"I do, yes. That was when your mood changed so dramatically."

"I looked out through the window of the cab, and saw the reason for the commotion. There is a ventilation shaft connecting to the Central London Railway which opens up into a grid in the pavement near Bond Street, and just as we were stopping next to it, a train must have blown past in the tunnel, for a stream of air suddenly came up through the grating and got hold of a lady's gown, resulting in rather an unseemly incident, if you take my meaning. The lady could not help but scream, and a couple of gentlemen rushed forward to remedy the problem before it had attracted too much notice. I saw it, however, and immediately I realised how Wilson had done it! A stream of air, or, in this case, gas, which is lighter than air, and would have the effect of turning the bed clothes into a balloon. But to anyone not aware of the actuality of it, it would be interpreted as a ghost. It is interesting, is it not, how even though ghosts do not exist, when we see its likeness, we instinctively assume it is one. In the words of the bard: 'Present fears are less than horrible imaginings.'"

"Watson?"

"Yes?"

"How do you hide something in an empty box?"

I looked up from my newspaper. Holmes was sitting on the other end of the breakfast table, going through the first post.

"How do you mean?"

"If I were to say to you that I had put something in a box, and you went and opened that box and found that it was empty, how would you account for it?"

I leaned back in my chair and gave the matter some thought. "Well, I suppose the only possible solution would be that you had hidden it in the walls of the box. Perhaps its insides are lined with cloth, and you have hidden whatever it is behind the cloth."

"Yes, that sounds reasonable, does it not?"

Holmes went back to studying a small piece of paper in his hand.

"What have you there?" I inquired.

"Oh, only a note that was sent to me. It concerns just such an empty box."

He pondered it for another short while, then tossed it to me across the table. I picked it up and read it:

"Dear Mr Holmes, I seek permission to visit you in the morning concerning a mystery that has puzzled me greatly of late. I am in possession of an old wooden box which is supposed to contain something very dear to me, but upon examination, the box proves empty. If you will see me, I would like to lay the matter before you and explain the details. Yours, M. Broker."

"Well, Watson." Holmes looked at me. "What say you?"

"It sounds intriguing."

"Yes. It is almost as if Mr Broker has gone out of the way to describe his problem so that it is certain to awaken my curiosity."

"Are you suspicious of it?"

"Well, the situation certainly raises a lot of questions. If the contents of the box are so precious to him, why does he not inspect the box in detail, perhaps even smashing it so as to see what is hidden in its walls?"

"Maybe the box is just as dear to him as its alleged content?"

"Yes. But the most likely hypothesis is probably that whatever he is looking for is not in the box at all. Theorising from so little information is useless, however. What more concrete conclusions can you draw from the letter?"

I turned the paper over a few times. "It is written in a neat hand, possibly that of an academic. It is curiously folded, which would indicate a man of eccentric qualities, and the strangely subservient tone of his writing adds to this impression. Apart from that, I think there is little to induce."

"And if I were to say to you that our Mr Broker is a man of an extremely nervous disposition, on what would you think I based that conclusion?" Holmes smiled as if he were a little devil.

I concentrated and examined the letter once more. "On the handwriting?"

"Precisely, Watson! Look at the careful and tidy printing. He has been writing so slowly and neatly that the shaking he is endeavouring to evade instead becomes visible in the unsteady appearance of his lines. At first glance, the writing is exquisite, and I would agree with you that our man is an academic, but he writes so slowly that, when scrutinised up close, the pen strokes look like little zigzag patterns." Holmes clapped his hands and bolted from his seat. "Now then! I believe our Mr Broker will be here any minute."

"You mean to say you've already answered his letter?"

"Of course. It arrived yesterday afternoon. I sent him a telegram last night. His letter was postmarked in Ealing, which would mean that if he went on the morning train from Ealing Broadway, he will be here within ten minutes."

And sure enough, only five had passed before we heard the sound of the bell and our visitor being greeted by the landlady. By then, Holmes and I had advanced from the breakfast table to the group of easy-chairs by the fire, and our leisurely dressing-gowns had been replaced by morning coats. The visitor was a robust type of medium height, looking much less the scholar than the athlete, and his shoulders were considerably broader than his waist. His face, however, was covered by a wild beard that lent him some of the air of the book-learning man.

"Mr Broker?" said Holmes.

"Masterman Broker at your service," said the man in a foghorn-like voice.

We introduced ourselves and the man was invited to sit down.

"I thank you for receiving me, gentlemen, although I know the matter that I described briefly in my letter to you may seem to be of a much too trivial nature to warrant your valuable time."

Holmes grabbed the armrests of his chair. "Trivial – yes. Uninteresting – absolutely not!"

"Well, perhaps you will see when I have explained further, that what appears trivial on the surface hides something very crucial."

"Such is, according to my experience, generally the case."

Broker's eyebrows changed into a formidable dark wall as his face assumed an air of gravity and he began his narrative:

"As I said, my name is Masterman Broker and I live in Ealing in a large detached villa in one of the suburb's leafier areas. I work as a school teacher and sometime private tutor, and am married since two years. I met my wife Eleanor while on a walking tour in the Swiss Alps, and we took an instant liking to each other. We are very happy together although our marriage is as yet childless. The house we live in is called Peregrine House and has belonged to my wife's family for some years. You see, it dates back to the time when that area was still just a country village, and since then suburban houses have sprung up all around it, altering the appearance of the district entirely. Since it is such a large house, and since my income is moderate, we live there together with my wife's brother and their elderly aunt, both their parents being deceased since a few years. In spite of this, we live comfortably and I get along very well with my brother-in-law. His name is George Falmer, and he works in the City. In fact, when I met my wife in Switzerland, she was holidaying there with him, so my acquaintance with George goes back just as far as my attachment to Eleanor.

"I tell you these things mainly to draw you a picture of my comfortable life and make you understand why the recent events strike me as so odd and inexplicable. Peregrine House lies surrounded by a large garden which has a high fence and thick shrubberies, making it virtually impossible for a thief to gain entrance to the house unnoticed. You see, I am not a wealthy man, and though my wife's father ran a prosperous shipping company which allowed him to build the house, their fortunes lie in the past. Therefore it came as a very welcome surprise to us all when I received the news that a distant cousin of my late father who emigrated to New Zealand at an early age and made a fortune in the gold rush of the '60s, is coming to London to spend his old age in his country of birth and settle his will which, as he made quite clear in his letter, will make me, being his only living relative, the sole benefactor. His letter was meticulous in its detailed instructions on how our meeting upon his arrival will be arranged, and how I will make myself conspicuous in order that he, having never met me before, will recognise me. The instructions involved me wearing a special type of flower native to New Zealand as a buttonhole, standing in a special pose, and other little eccentric details that I cannot now recall.

"I will now explain to you as clearly as I may how this vital letter disappeared right under my very nose. I am in the habit of opening my letters in my study, a large murky chamber that used to belong to my wife's father. The contents of that room are mainly his old things, including his desk, his chair, his bookcases, and a small sideboard upon which stands an old wooden box which I believe is of oriental manufacture. It was given to him as a present from one of his associates and everyone who has seen it ensures me that it is most exquisite and probably quite valuable. My father-in-law was in the habit of keeping valuable documents in it, and I have taken up the tradition. Yesterday afternoon I was in the study together with George, who sometimes keeps me company after coming back from work. We were chatting about commonplace matters while I dealt with my correspondence, and suddenly I had in my hand the letter from Uncle Bertrand. I read it to myself while George impatiently wondered why I had gone quiet. When I had finished reading it carefully, I explained to him in outline what it had said. He reacted in his usual rumbustious way, getting up from his chair, congratulating and embracing me. Realising that everything depended upon this letter, the instructions it contained and my uncle's demand that I produce it upon our meeting as a final proof that I am who I claim to be, I grew anxious and wanted to hide it.

"George calmed me, walked across the room to the sideboard and took the oriental box. He brought it over to the desk and lifted the lid.

"'This old thing has proved trustworthy for a long time,' he said.

"I tossed the letter into the box.

George closed the lid and carried it back to the sideboard. Then he turned to me with a beaming smile. 'I will run down to the corner and pick up a bottle of champagne!'

"I smiled in response and he disappeared from the room. I sat there in my chair for a good while, pondering the sudden fortune that had fallen upon me. Then I began to nurture feelings of apprehension, and an impulse made me rise from my chair and walk over to the box. I knew I would feel a lot safer if the letter was in the inside pocket of my jacket. It was not that I doubted the safety of the box, but I knew that once I had left the room, I would start feeling nervous. Furthermore, there is no way of locking the box. In the unlikely event of a burglary, the letter was completely exposed.

"I lifted the lid, and what I saw filled me with horror and confusion. The box was empty! Inside it was nothing but the bottom and four walls of rough wood. I had put the letter there myself. I had seen it lying on the bottom before George closed the lid. There is no way it could have disappeared. I ran out into the hallway and managed to stop George before he went out. He came back and together we examined the box and searched the floor of the study, but to no avail. The celebratory glass of champagne instead became a calming glass of brandy."

Mr Broker sank back into his chair with an expression of sorrow, as if relating the events had made him relive the emotional process all over again. I was as puzzled by the story as the man himself, but one possibility struck me.

"How trustworthy is your brother-in-law?" I asked.

"I have prepared myself for the eventuality that such a question would arise," said he, "as I suppose that would be the most probable solution to someone who hears the story without being part of it. But I assure you, gentlemen, that I have complete confidence in him. He has become to me something of the brother I never had. As to the scenario of him purloining the letter through some feat of dexterity, I can only say to you that that is not a possibility. I put the letter into the box myself, he closed it without touching the inside of the box, and the box has no holes nor can it be opened in any other way than through the top lid. The box never left my sight. The whole thing is simply impossible."

"Tell us more about the box itself," enquired Holmes.

Mr Broker shrugged his shoulders. "There is not much to tell. It is shaped like a cube, about fifteen inches wide and fifteen inches deep. The outside has some carvings that have been smoothed out with age. The inside of it is undecorated, however, and apart from the decorations it is quite simple and unadorned. I have no knowledge of antiques, but to me it seems to be the work of a common village artisan, and I doubt that it would fetch a high price at an auction."

Abruptly, Holmes drew his legs up into the chair he was reclining in, changing his position into that of a Buddha. He pressed his fingertips together and pointed them at our client. "Mr Broker. Since so much of this problem hangs upon what

169

happened between your putting the letter in the box and your reopening of the box, it is of the utmost necessity that you think hard about those few seconds and tell us any details about what occurred in them that might have bearing upon the case."

Holmes spoke slowly and severely, and Mr Broker evidently appreciated the gravity of his words, for he thought long and hard before saying anything. "There is nothing. I did not look away from the box even for a second, of that I am certain. George turned from the desk, the box in his hands, and walked the few paces to the sideboard. I think he stumbled on the edge of the carpet that lies in front of the desk, but there was no more drama to it than that."

"I understand. What exactly is it that Mr Falmer does in the City?"

Mr Broker looked uncomfortable upon hearing the question. "I believe he works for a stockbroker's firm called Sanderson & Cox. I have little knowledge of the type of work he does there, but I understand that he is highly thought of by his superiors, and his wages were recently increased."

"That sounds both dull and interesting at the same time," replied Holmes. "Are he and his sister very close?"

"Oh yes. Before I came into the picture, they only had each other. Eleanor is George's senior by three years, and that makes her a bit domineering in their relationship. George, on the other hand, has the role of the raucous impulsive youth, but in a harmless way, and he infuses a sense of humour into their relationship which makes it very sympathetic."

"You do not happen to have a picture of your brother-in-law on you, do you?"

Broker raised his eyebrows, and hesistated for a moment. "I am not in the habit of carrying photographs of every male acquaintance on my person."

"Then maybe you will give us a brief description of what he looks like?" insisted Holmes.

"I really do not understand what purpose that will serve."

"Simply trust me, Mr Broker. The whole case may depend upon it."

He sighed and did what Holmes had asked of him. "George is medium height, slim, fair-haired, with side whiskers and a moustache. His most distinguishing feature is his right forefinger which misses its outer phalanx as the result of a childhood injury."

"Excellent, Mr Broker, that should do."

"Any more questions?"

"What about the old aunt?" I said.

"She has passed ninety and lives in a room on the top floor from which she rarely ventures. She is hard of hearing and exceedingly forgetful. I cannot possibly think that she has anything to do with this."

"We can be sure of nothing at this point, Mr Broker," said Holmes in my defence. "My experience tells me that a thief can be in another room than where the theft takes place and still be guilty."

"That sounds incredible," said Broker.

"Ha! Do you not recall, Watson, the curious case of the Smithers jewels?"

I could not keep from slapping my knee. "By Jove, Holmes, you're right!"

"And how was it perpetrated?" asked Broker.

"By an intricate system of strings connected via the bell-ropes," replied Holmes. "The diligence and patience of thieves are not to be underestimated, Mr Broker!"

"Good. Now then, Mr Holmes, I was hoping that you and Dr Watson might want to accompany me back to Ealing to examine the box and my study. I was uncertain about whether I should bring the box here, but from what I have read about your exploits, I gathered that you might want to look at it in situ, as it were. Since the letter is evidently not in the box, the obvious object of your examinations I suppose should be the room instead."

"That is wise of you, but it is also unfortunate that you have left the box and the room unguarded."

"My wife is there."

"Yes, of course. And your brother-in-law?"

"We went into town together. He continued to his office."

"I see. And when will he be back?"

"Late this afternoon."

"Good. We will come to Ealing, Mr Broker, but I would implore you to go back on your own and stay at your house keeping the box under constant supervision until we get there."

"Why will you not come with me now?"

"Because there are certain points in this case that I would like to satisfy myself on first. Make sure that your wife is in the house, and stay with your wife in your study. Watson and I will be there no later than three o'clock this afternoon, and then I hope to be able to present a solution."

"I have little faith of recovering my letter, but I appreciate your help and am thankful for it."

"Rest assured, Mr Broker, that all is not lost."

Holmes saw our visitor, who looked slightly relieved but also puzzled, to the door. When he was just about to leave, Holmes stopped him.

"By the way, Mr Broker. What was the name of your wife's father?"

Broker looked back at Holmes with a blank gaze. "Frederick Falmer," he said.

"Thank you," said Holmes and shut the door in his face.

I looked at my friend with a mixture of amusement and indignation as he walked up to the fireplace and lit a cigarrette. He leaned towards the mantelpiece and shot me a glance. "Fascinating, wouldn't you say?"

"Fascinating, yes, in its impossibility."

Holmes chuckled. "Yes, it's strange, is it not, how little everyday objects can baffle us so? Nevertheless, I will wager that the key to it all rests in one of the little details that Mr Broker has provided us with."

"But why were you so keen to know what his brother-in-law looks like?"

"That, my dear friend, is precisely the information I needed for the little excursion I am about to do now!"

"Oh I see. Hush hush, eh? And I assume you do not want me to accompany you?"

Holmes smiled and I understood at once that, as usual, he felt the need to be secretive until he could be positive that his conjectures were correct.

"But I hope," he said, "that you will accompany me to Ealing this afternoon?"

I tried to look as secretive as him, and failed.

"Of course!" I said.

Holmes was gone no more than an hour, after which he returned to Baker Street invigorated and in good spirits. I had passed the time in solitude by trying to contemplate the problem that had been laid before us that morning, but was dissatisfied with my conclusions. The best possibility I could think of was that the letter had somehow slipped between a crack in the bottom of the box that had been invisible in the murkiness of Broker's study, and I presented this hypothesis to Holmes when he returned.

"I think," he replied, "that you are staring yourself blind on the events of that isolated study. When you have a case like this, all trapped within the minutiae of a small incident in a closed space, you must not forget the context. Context is everything, my dear Watson! Would Louis XVI have been beheaded if it had not been for the revolutionary atmosphere of eighteenth-century Paris?"

"I suppose not."

"Of course not, my boy! To conceive of the execution of a king as a murder perpetrated by a man who happens to work as an executioner would be to foolishly ignore obvious instrumental circumstances."

"And what have you been doing then?" I asked.

"I have been looking into the affairs of two men – Frederick and George Falmer."

"And what have you discovered?"

"Vital things. The main point of which I suppose is that Frederick Falmer is the same person as Fiddly Freddy."

"Fiddly Freddy?"

"You do not recall him?"

"I cannot say that I do."

"Well, perhaps you were not such an avid music-hall visitor in your youth. Fiddly Freddy was one of the most successful performers of the London music halls a few decades ago."

"I thought Mrs. Broker's father was in shipping?"

"It sounds more respectable, does it not? Especially if you want to set up house in a fashionable middle-class suburb. But I tell you, Watson, that Fiddly Freddy is the key to the whole thing! But we have no time to lose. We must get to Ealing before any danger befalls our client."

What type of danger was in store, or why Holmes had taken a sudden interest in old music-hall performers, I had no idea, but I took my hat and coat and followed him without hesitation, and within half an hour we were walking through the pleasant autumn landscape of the western London suburb.

Peregrine House was a forbidding red-brick building located at the end of one of the common suburban streets, but set apart from the rest of the homely-looking villas by its worn and archaic appearance, and by the surrounding wilderness of a garden, which only allowed the passer-by to see the very top of the building from the street. We were welcomed into the house by a dirty-aproned chambermaid who quickly scurried off to fetch her master. The entrance hall showed signs of a vulgar taste – the traces of upstart characteristics in the man who once built the edifice, I thought to myself. Masterman Broker soon descended the grand staircase to greet us, arm-in-arm with his wife, a pleasant young lady with kind eyes and dimpled cheeks.

"I am so glad to see you again," he said. "There has been no change in the matter since we last spoke."

"Well, let's see if we cannot put a right to that," said Holmes.

And with a brisk step, he started to go up the stairs ahead of us all. The Brokers hurried after, and Mr Broker managed to catch up with him in order to direct him to the study. We were shown to a closed door down the corridor on the first floor, and Holmes took hold of the handle.

"When are you expecting Mr Falmer back?" he asked.

"In about half an hour, perhaps," said Mrs. Broker.

Holmes nodded and opened the door. The room was dark and slightly overfurnished, with bookcases lining the walls and a vast rug spreading from the threshold to the large desk at the far end. The curtains were drawn, and a small table lamp on the desk provided the only illumination. In front of the desk were two visitor's chairs, and along the booklined walls were placed a few sideboards upon which a selection of exotic or decorative trinkets had been arranged. One of these tables had on it only one object, a medium-sized old wooden box.

"Ah! I assume this is what has been giving you trouble?" said Holmes, approaching it.

Broker sighed and nodded.

"Well, well, well." Holmes picked it up and looked at it closely. Then he put it down again and lifted the lid. He peered down for a long time, slowly leaning down lower and lower, until his face was almost inside the box. Then with a sudden movement he looked up at us again. He smiled and motioned at us to come closer. We all assembled around the box. Holmes looked at us, barely able to contain his giddiness, and then he put his hand in the box. He fumbled around at the bottom for a while, and then all of a sudden there was a change in his face as if he had found something.

"Now," he said, "if you will please look closely at the bottom of the box."

His fingers were placed along the edge of the bottom and with a delicate motion, they slowly lifted the bottom as if it was itself a lid. Lifting it higher, he managed to hold it more firmly, and when it was fully opened, this false bottom became one wall of the box, thin enough not to make the wall that was already there noticeably thicker. But what was even more extraordinary, was that the lifting of the bottom had revealed a piece of folded-up paper that had been lying underneath it.

Holmes picked it up. "Is this your letter, Mr Broker?"

Broker stared at the letter, his eyes wide open, and his only response was a faint nod. Mrs. Broker smiled and put her hand on her husband's shoulder. He took the letter and examined it.

"Yes," he said. "This is certainly it! Do you mean to tell me it was there all the time? But how… and how did you know where to look?"

Holmes picked up the box once more.

"Have a look at this. See the ornaments and the carvings? Yes, the style is decidedly oriental, but this was not made in the orient. It was made by someone who have seen some pictures of oriental decoration, at best, but who is, on the whole, quite a mediocre artisan. I should say this was made in Croydon."

"Croydon?" I exclaimed incredulously.

"There is a workshop out in Croydon that specialises in the construction of devices for magicians."

"Magicians?" said Broker.

"Of course!" I said. "Fiddly Freddy."

"Dear God," said Mrs. Broker.

We all turned towards her.

"Yes," she said. "I should have realised. This 'magic' box was one of my father's contraptions that he used for one of his routines. He was a music-hall conjurer."

"He was?" cried Broker. "But I thought…"

"Father was always ashamed of the way he made his fortune. Coming from such a simple background as he did, he was always anxious to escape his humble beginnings, not to mention hide them from his family. Both George and I were raised in this house after he had settled down and left the stage for good. I was unaware that he had kept any of the props he used as a performer, seeing as he wanted to leave it all behind him, but maybe he was more nostalgic than I thought."

"I conducted some research this morning," declared Holmes, "going through back editions of *The Era*. You see, when Mr Broker mentioned his father-in-law's name to me, I recognised it instantly as the real name of 'Fiddly Freddy', the music-hall conjurer. And this to me seemed a vital point. I managed to find several reviews of his appearances, some of which mentioned his use of the 'The Vortex of Arabia', an oriental box in which any item that was placed there disappeared without a trace. One of the reviewers looked through the trick, however, and noticed how Freddy, when the person he had called up from the audience had put something in the box, carried it across the stage before opening it, and when doing so, pretended to stumble on a floor board. Making some witty remark about this apparently indeliberate faux-pas, he continued by opening the box, revealing it to be inexplicably empty. It was while reading this account that I remembered one detail from your story, Mr Broker."

"That George stumbled on the edge of the carpet!" said Broker.

"Precisely. Mrs. Broker, just how well acquainted was your brother with your father's past?"

The woman shook her head anxiously.

"George did spend a lot of time with father in this room when he was young. But why would he…?"

Just then a man appeared in the doorframe. He was tall and elegant, and he smiled a world-weary smile at us. "Hello, what's going on here?"

Mrs. Broker stepped up to him. "George, can you explain this? Masterman's letter was in the box the whole time!"

Mr Falmer looked at his sister, then at us and then at the box. "Well, I never. What an extraordinary thing!"

"Come, come, Mr Falmer," said Holmes. "Such charades are only a waste of time."

"Charades? I'm sure I have no idea what you are talking about."

"Did you know this box was one of father's old magic boxes?" enquired Mrs. Broker.

Falmer walked up to it and examined it. "How curious."

His sister turned impatiently to Holmes. "Oh, I cannot stand this, Mr Holmes. Do you really mean to imply that George hid the letter on purpose?"

"On purpose?" said Falmer. "Balderdash!"

Holmes raised his hands in a gesture of appeasement.

"Please, Mr Falmer, it is no good. I know that you took advantage of the box and its hidden mechanism in order to hide the letter."

"That is a gross accusation, sir! You have no proof."

"I do. Earlier today I visited the offices of the firm where you work, Sanderson & Cox."

"Did you?"

"I did. Or at least I tried to, seeing as how the firm was dissolved two months ago."

"What?" exclaimed Mrs. Broker.

"The man I spoke to in the neighbouring office," Holmes continued, "had some interesting things to say about you, Mr Falmer, and the gambling debts that you would have such difficulty paying back without an employment."

"This is utter nonsense!" said the accused man, and sat himself down in one of the chairs.

"Mr Holmes makes rather a plausible case to me," said Masterman Broker severely.

"But let us not get ahead of ourselves," Holmes remarked. "In all likeliness, the whole affair was thought up impulsively.

You were with Mr Broker as he opened his letter, just as you had been in this room with your father all those years ago, and considering your delicate predicament, the plan to hide the letter with the help of the box and then snatch it when the box was left unguarded must have come to you abruptly. I knew that we had to act swiftly while you were in the City, or wherever it is you go during the days, before you came back and had an opportunity to take the letter."

"But how on earth could you guess that this was the solution?" asked Broker.

"I never guess, Mr Broker. I realised from your narrative that the answer was to be found in the box and that Mr Falmer's behaviour was suspicious. Until I had looked into Mr Falmer and his job, I could not be certain of anything, of course. Your description of him served me well while making enquiries. Mr Falmer is well known in many of the gambling halls frequented by City clerks. When I learned the true identity of his father, the pieces of the puzzle started to fit together, and I realised that Mr Falmer had copied one of his father's old routines by pretending to stumble on the edge of the carpet, thereby hiding how he shaked the box to make the false bottom fall down and hide the letter."

"Ingenious!" I could not help exclaiming.

"Father was most creative," Mrs. Broker conceded.

"The question is," Holmes resumed, "how far Mr Falmer's plans developed. Did he regret his trick immediately afterwards and decide to return the letter, or did his plan involve something more sinister, perhaps even murder? For if he meant to impersonate his brother-in-law when meeting Uncle Bertrand, he would have to make sure that Mr Broker would not be there to thwart his scheme."

Our eyes turned in unison towards Mr Falmer, who was looking much less confident than he had when entering the room and claiming his innocence. "I can only ask you to believe me when I say that I had the idea then and there, but that I did not realise what it would entail if I were to follow it through. I have been in hell since I lost my job and was unable to pay back my gambling debts, and only a desperate man could think of a plan that would mean going behind the back of the two people in the world he loves the most. Oh, Eleanor, Masterman! As soon as I grasped the full meaning of what I had done, I promised myself that I would take out the letter and hand it back to you. In fact, that is just what I was about to do when I came in here."

I need hardly describe to you the idyll of reconciliation that ensued. The words and gestures that passed in the last act of this drama must remain the private dominion of the principal players. I can only say that Holmes and I were escorted from Peregrine House in an atmosphere of gratitude and relief, Mr Broker promising that his brother-in-law would surely benefit from the money obtained from Uncle Betrand. We then enjoyed a leisurely stroll through Ealing as a reward for our brief but intensive day's work. We had walked along in silence for a few minutes, when my friend surprised me with an unexpected comment:

"I must say, my dear Watson, that I am indebted to you."

"To me? How so?"

"Don't you remember me asking you about how you hide something in an empty box this morning?"

"I do, but I cannot recall my answer."

"You said that it must be in the walls of the box, which initially put me on the right line of reasoning. I thought to myself then that if something goes missing in a box it must be, not inside the box, but *inside* the box, if you get my meaning."

"I certainly do, Holmes, but you flatter me. I was only speculating."

"Sometimes I think that what I do consciously, you do unconsciously. And I do not know that my method is the preferable one."

The Adventure of the Migrating Monocle

"When you have eliminated the impossible, whatever remains, however improbable, must be the truth." This maxim, which was one of the guiding principles of Sherlock Holmes' working methods, I have had occasion to reiterate in a number of the chronicles of my good friend's exploits. In no other case that came our way in the years in which Holmes was active, though, was this sentiment more put to the test than in that most improbable affair of Mr Gregory Furniss and the curious disappearance and reappearance of his monocle. For perhaps more than any other problem that came in our path, it demonstrated just how improbable that last remaining possibility can be, and that our world is, as Holmes so often stated, extraordinary enough without the addition of the supernatural.

The case was first brought to our attention by Mycroft Holmes, who summoned Holmes and me to the Diogenes Club one morning in late April, by way of a very brief telegram.

"'Come to the Diogenes at once and lunch is on me. Wish to consult you on a matter of the utmost urgency.' Ha!" Holmes exclaimed as he read it aloud to me, before he tossed it into his empty armchair and continued pacing the room. "My dear brother seems to think I am able to drop everything and come to him whenever he calls."

"But you have no case at present," I replicated.

"It is the arrogance that provokes, rather than the timing. Mycroft's scope is so narrow that, to him, every concern that comes his way is 'of the utmost urgency'. If he would step outside his comfortable club once in a while, he might feel compelled to express himself with less embroidery."

"Nevertheless, his summons often mean rewarding cases. He has the same criteria for what makes an interesting problem as you. The last time he called, he put us on the track of that curious business of the three Japanese sailors."

Holmes picked up the bow of his violin from the table by the window, then put it down again. "He could at least have given us some clue as to what it concerns."

I smiled inwardly at this effervescent display of brotherly bickering, and knew full well that Mycroft avoided details in his telegram to arouse his brother's curiosity – a method that I knew would work. The two had developed a discourse of interaction that emanated from their awareness that the one could always deduce the other's intentions, thus deliberately keeping information from each other, but disclosing enough to ensure that contact never broke down. Not many minutes had passed, then, before Holmes and I were in a hansom on our way to Pall Mall, and the pleasant environment of the Diogenes Club.

Mycroft immediately escorted us into a private dining room, where we were introduced to Gregory Furniss, one of his fellow members. Furniss' appearance struck me instantly as that of the most suave and garish young swell. His dress was immaculate and expertly tailored, but had just that inkling of exaggeration in its style that bordered on vulgarity. It was little things: a plaid waistcoat, an unusually thick watch-chain, a long thin walking-stick that he leaned on to make his posture more elegant, and, to top it all, in his right eye there sat a monocle of octagonal shape. "Here is a parvenu," I thought to myself. A man whose upward mobility had received a glowing start by membership to the Diogenes Club. But why would Mycroft Holmes be rubbing shoulders with a man like that? I glanced at Holmes as we greeted them, trying to read his

184

reaction to Mr Furniss in his facial expression, but he did not give away anything, and as we began our meal and Furniss laid his problem before us in a delicate and humble voice, I thought that maybe his looks were deceiving.

"I wished to consult you, Mr Holmes," he said, "on rather a delicate matter and I trust that what I will say to you will go no further than this room. It is relevant to my problem that I am currently preparing a career in politics, to try and continue the great work of my late father, whose membership at this club I was kindly allowed to inherit."

I was surprised to hear that this was the explanation of his membership, and the fact that his flamboyant appearance was not attributable to an upstart background made me conclude that I was simply out of touch with the way young people dressed.

"My political ambitions," he continued, "are still not widely known, but some of the more disreputable newspapers have been able to guess it based on the gossip of Whitehall, and this has made some of the old enemies of my father smell the scent of blood. I therefore suspected that someone would try to thwart my plans before they had come to fruition."

"The political game is an ugly one, Sherlock," added Mycroft. "Too ugly for the likes of you and me."

Holmes nodded and turned his gaze back on Furniss.

"My suspicions were realised two days ago. This is what happened. I spent my boyhood and youth at the Norfolk country house of my family, and only a year ago, following the untimely death of my father and my decision to take up politics, did I move permanently to London. I soon understood that a serious political career required me to take part in the social life of parliamentarians and civil servants in the metropolis, fraternising in the clubs of St James's and the bars of Mayfair. In time, I took to this life, gradually immersing into the culture of both the Burlington Arcade dandies and Belgravia society. I have managed to find a way of combining the vigour of the young swell with the tradition and confidence of the political establishment in a way that I think will appeal to a new generation of voters. My entrance into this world was assisted in no small way through the close collaboration I had with my Conduit Street tailor. In spite of this success, however, my rural upbringing has always been at the back of my mind, and often are the moments when, in the privacy of my parlour, my thoughts go back to the open fields and idyllic farms of home. To ease this nostalgia, I recently took to making nocturnal walks in some of the less prosperous areas of London, where the down-to-earth character of village life is more tangible. My preferred area of relaxation is Rotherhithe, where some of the areas of wharves and low brick buildings remind me of the fishing villages on the east coast. I have found a lovely little tavern, housed in a building lying close to the river, catering to the local warehouse porters and boat proprietors, and it has become something of a ritual for me to take refuge in this place at least once a week as a counterweight to all the snobbery and camaraderie of the West End. I sit in a quiet booth in the back, away from the commotion at the counter, have a pot of ale or two and eat a hearty country meal of sausage and mash.

"Three days ago, however, on Monday, I had a strange experience at this tavern. I was scheduled to speak in the evening at a banquet held on account of the Belgian state visit. The event will mark a considerable upturn in the course of my career, but in advance, the prospect filled me with dread. Before the occasion, however, I had a few hours to myself, and in order to relieve some of the tensions, I decided to go to

Rotherhithe and my favourite place of refuge from the bustle of high politics. The banquet was to commence at eight o'clock. I was at the tavern around half past six, which gave me just enough time to relax in my booth with a drink. Now, as you see, I make use of a monocle. It is an aide for the impaired vision in my right eye, but it has also become something of a recognisable trait for me, especially as I am in the habit of wearing octagonal monocles of special manufacture from the firm of Warburton on Sackville Street. I have been advised to continue wearing these characteristic glasses as a politician, as it will make me instantly recognisable, and, according to some, will make me known by the nickname of Mr Octagon." Furniss smiled self-consciously at this. "It is neither here nor there with me, so I have become accustomed to wearing them. When I relax in my booth at the Rotherhithe tavern, however, I tend to dislodge my monocle and place it on the table in front of me. I did exactly that this Monday, and when I had finished my beer and was preparing to leave, the monocle was gone. It was no great loss, but the strange traceless disappearance annoyed me, and so I searched for it as carefully as I could on the darkened floor of the interior. But it was nowhere to be seen. I have several others, supplied to me on a regular basis by Mr Warburton, and so I did not make too much of it then and there, as by now I had to hurry so as not to be late for the banquet, at which I arrived just in the nick of time.

"The problem started the next day. My valet awoke me in the morning with a note that had just arrived for me. The person who had delivered it had been a seedy character, and he had said that the message was of great urgency. I sat up in bed, drank some water from the glass by my bedside to clear my head, and read the note. I have it with me." Furniss produced a folded piece of paper from his inside pocket and proceeded by reciting its content. "'Mr Furniss, if you wish to retrieve your missing monocle, you may do so by refraining from any contact with the authorities or the police and pay a sum of £50,000 to the sender of this letter. The monocle was found by the police at precisely seven o'clock on Monday night during a raid of a house of ill repute in the vicinity of Wapping. It has been confiscated by the administering superintendent together with other items found on the premises, noting the exact time of discovery. As you have no alibi for this point in time, there will be no reason to suppose any other scenario than that you were present in that house before attending the banquet at Whitehall, once the police are informed of the ownership of the monocle. Since the monocle is unique in design and manufacture, there will be no use in opposing this information. Should you wish to save your promising career from the blemish of scandal, we advise you to follow the instructions that will be sent to you shortly.' The letter is signed with a capital D."

"Will you please give me the letter and the envelope?" asked Holmes.

"You will not be able to deduce much, Sherlock," remarked Mycroft. "We are dealing with refined blackmailers here. The letter is carefully stripped of all useful data, as if they knew it would somehow come your way."

"Quite right. Run-of-the-mill stationary, east London postmark, written on a cheap typewriter with a characteristic flaw in the i's. And I'll warrant that the man who delivered it was a hired hand who knows nothing of this. Have any other communiqués reached you?"

"Yes," replied Furniss. "This morning I received this."

He handed over an identical envelope, addressed and stamped in just the same way. Holmes read the note.

"'Have the money ready in bank notes this Friday. We will contact you.' Hum! They are exceedingly professional and to the point. Yes, this is an experienced gang. You will notice of course that they stress the time when the monocle was found by the police. This is the strong point of their hold on you, Mr Furniss, since you have no reliable witness to testify that you were in the tavern at that time. They took advantage of the fact that you sneaked off to Rotherhithe just before the banquet, when you were in the company of hundreds of witnesses and there would be no point in trying to incriminate you. This means that they have followed your movements for some time until they were sure that your excursions to Rotherhithe would form an admirable basis for the blackmailing project. Making sure that nobody in your surroundings knew of your Rotherhithe visits would necessitate other sources of information too, but your being a public figure and a man of many contacts, I suppose this is not difficult."

"Mr Holmes," said Furniss, "I simply cannot understand how my monocle was removed from my booth at the tavern and transported to a brothel on the other side of the river in the matter of minutes!"

"Unless the blackmailers are bluffing?" I said.

"I have made some preliminary inquiries," said Mycroft, "including an unofficial visit to the Wapping police station where a superintendent Croft is compiling his report of the raid as we speak. The monocle is in the possession of the police. I have seen it with my own eyes, and Croft himself swears that it was found in this seedy place at seven on Monday evening."

"And this monocle is absolutely unique?" asked Holmes.

"Without a doubt," said Furniss. "I have Warburton's solemn promise that the design is individual and that he would not sell that type to any other customers."

"The man makes spectacles to many prominent people," added Mycroft. "His word is reliable."

"An octagonal monocle," I said, "is unusual, but not unheard of. Can it not be a forgery?"

"I compared the specimen at the police station with one that Furniss gave me. The shape is special, every alternate side cut long and the others cut a bit shorter, with a frosted edge."

"The drawback of trying to be distinctive," said Holmes. "An ordinary man is more difficult to link to the scene of a crime."

"Furniss came to me the day before yesterday asking for my help in this matter," said Mycroft. "As I was a close friend and associate of his father's, I did not hesitate to try and do what I can for the lad. I went to the police station to verify the information of the letter, but more than that I am afraid is beyond what my busy schedule allows. I have no time to make inquiries in Rotherhithe! It is a case that I know will interest you, however, my dear brother."

Holmes smiled at Mycroft with a suggestion of prickliness in his eye. "Mr Furniss," he said, "is there anybody you can think of who might have the motive or capability to try and frame you like this? You mentioned some old enemies of your father?"

"Well, it is no secret that my father was a staunch liberal, and his opinions naturally instigated some debate. The one man who suffered the most damage to his career from the actions of my father was probably Sheldon Carmichael, the then MP for Burnley, whose corrupt dealings with a dishonest builder in a housing project for the poor was revealed to the public as a result of my father's investigations, ruining Carmichael both financially and politically."

"Where is this Carmichael fellow now?"

"He has regained some of his former reputation," said Mycroft, "and now holds quite a prominent position within the Conservative Party."

"I see. And the prospect of a Furniss junior rising to eminence may have caused him to fear for his future."

"But I cannot see how he could have orchestrated this!" complained Furniss. "Least of all I cannot grasp how they have proof that I was in a completely different place than where I was."

Holmes lowered his face and gazed at Furniss through the tangle of his brow. "Mr Furniss, if this situation becomes more delicate than it already is, just how prepared are you to publicly admit your visits to Rotherhithe to avert scandal?"

"If every Englishman saw it the way I did there would be no problem with that. But I know that a right honourable gentleman eating meat pies in a pub in Rotherhithe does not look good. It is slightly better, however, than a politician in a low house in Wapping. But I beg you, Mr Holmes, to do what you can before we consider this possibility!"

"You have my assurance of that, Mr Furniss."

Mycroft gestured contentedly. "Then you take the case? Splendid! What do you propose to do first?"

Holmes sipped his wine in thought.

"A natural line of inquiry would be to find out who tipped the police off about the brothel in Wapping. Superintendent Croft is an old friend. But before we leave, could you please tell me, Mr Furniss, as precisely as possible at what time you saw that your monocle was missing?"

Furniss took the question seriously, and thought for a long while. "A quarter to seven. Yes, I remember the bells of St Mary's striking three quarters. That was what made me look up from my drink."

191

"Thank you, Mr Furniss. And now, gentlemen, I bid you good day."

We took leave of our lunch party, and Holmes promised to report on his progress to Furniss before the end of the day.

"What are your impressions of Gregory Furniss?" I asked Holmes as we were in a hansom rattling in the direction of Wapping.

"An endearing fellow, don't you think?"

"He is a snob!"

"A simple country boy trying to keep up with the smart set of the metropolis but displaying his exclusion to those who can detect the details. He tries just a bit too hard, does he not? It reveals his humanity. Not to mention that speech impediment."

"His speech was perfect."

"Exactly. But most of all I see a fellow flâneur in the impulse that drives him to visit Rotherhithe. Have you been, Watson? It is a most refreshing place when you grow tired of delicate maidens and dignified gents. I go there now and then, but unlike our Mr Furniss I take the precaution of assuming a disguise. All this of course springs from the carelessness of moving about in such an area dressed as a Mayfair dandy."

"You think his presence aroused provocation?"

"I think that, by discovering these excursions, his enemies found a weak spot that they considered a suitable basis for blackmail."

"Then why not simply obtain some evidence of his presence in Rotherhithe and blackmail him with that?"

"It is not aggravating enough. He can easily explain it away by claiming to do charity work or some such business. But it was a weak spot in that it brought him close to a dark and dangerous world. It would have been easy to snatch away something of his and plant it in a nearby house of revelry. The choice of the monocle was inspired, and cannot have been accidental. They knew beforehand that it was unique and would be seen as unquestionable proof of his presence. They probably chose the closest such house to the tavern."

"The only problem being that it was on the other side of the river."

"Yes, and this does not seem to have constituted an obstacle to them, which I would consider the most promising starting point for our enquiry. But Wapping police station is coming up on our right side. Come, Watson! Let us hope the superintendent is in."

Superintendent Thomas Croft was a long and thin man, unusual for a uniformed policeman, and he was glad to see Holmes, with whom he seemed to have cooperated before the commencement of my acquaintance with him. He showed us into a cramped and unadorned office room, where he produced a wooden box from a shelf upon which several similar containers lay. Opening it upon a desk, he explained it as holding the items that had been confiscated at the raid. Among the numerous objects were articles of clothing, tiepins and silk handkerchiefs which gave a picture of the class of clients at that place of debauchery. In the bottom lay the monocle, which, in the same way as the other smaller items, had been placed in a brown envelope.

"Where exactly was it found?" asked Holmes.

"In one of the back rooms, on top of a bed," replied Croft.

"Had the bed been slept in?"

I could not help but blush at Holmes' indelicate query, but the superintendent retained his composure.

"No. It was covered by a large bedthrow."

"I see."

Holmes studied the eyeglass closely, first scrutinising the expertly cut octagonal glass itself, then holding up the piece of cord that was tied to a little ring in its corner. "The monocle does not show any signs of damage, which is most noteworthy. The only blemish is halfway down the cord, where it is frayed slightly. This piece of evidence has been handled with the utmost care. Tell me, superintendent, how did this raid come about? Did you receive an anonymous tip?"

"Actually, we did not. This operation had been planned for weeks, ever since our men on the beat started to report seeing suspicious comings and goings to and from that house."

"How secret were your plans?"

Croft probably gathered that Holmes suspected a stool pigeon, but affected innocence. "It was of course only known to my men, but as you know there is never any guarantee. Some of them are not averse to a drink, and might well have spilled the beans as a result of it."

"Thank you, superintendent! You needn't worry. This case is much too substantial for any criticisms of your work to play a major part in it. We would now be extremely grateful to you if we could inspect the scene of the raid."

"It is not far from here, which is ironic, I suppose. I will have one of my constables escort you."

A police constable called Brody showed us down the street, into a confusing jumble of narrow alleyways, and then out into a backstreet dwarfed on one side by a large warehouse. Here the immoral house lay, its unassuming exterior disguised as a seedy private dwelling. Brody unlocked the door and turned up the gas as we stepped in, throwing light upon a surprisingly garlanded front room, presumably made to look as inviting as possible in this part of the city to distinguished clients from its other part. We were taken up a small flight of stairs to a corridor whose shabby character contrasted with the decoration of the ground floor.

"This is the room," said Brody, opening one of the doors.

It was a small and simple bedroom, occupied by a wide bed, a touch too large, with a washstand, a minuscule dressing-table and tattered crimson curtains hiding a window. Holmes stepped up to it and pushed away the curtain with a single motion of the hand. The glittering surface of the Thames was just below. Quickly, as if caught by a sudden bout of curiosity, he pulled open the window and leaned out. I walked up to him to see what he saw, and was nearly overcome by dizziness when I saw that the house we were in was perched quite high on wooden posts plunging straight into the black waters of the river.

Holmes turned around and looked at the constable. "At precisely what time did the raid commence?" he asked.

Brody produced his official notebook. "We entered the premises at exactly nine minutes to seven."

"And how long did it take you to advance into this room?"

"Not more than six or seven minutes."

"That should be about right. The time written on the envelope at the station was 6.57."

"That means," I interjected, "that it came here from the tavern in Rotherhithe in less than a quarter of an hour."

"Which is impossible," said Holmes, looking strangely pleased with this observation.

"A fast cab ride here from Rotherhithe," remarked Brody, "takes at least half an hour."

I looked out of the window again. "I have it! They brought it across in a boat. A steam launch would do the journey in that time."

"At the same time drawing much attention to itself in this quiet corner of Wapping," said Holmes. "A rowing boat would take much more than half an hour in this current. But the main thing that excludes the eventuality of a boat is the height of this window. That wall is impossible to scale."

I could not but admit that he was right. "Then how was it carried out?"

Holmes glanced out the window again, peering into the distance as if he was looking for something. "Cunningly," he replied. "Most cunningly."

He remained silent during our cab ride back to Baker Street, and persisted with this reticence as he shrouded himself in his blue dressing-gown and took his position by the fire with his reliable briar, the pipe that he used for the most critical moments in his investigations. I knew him well enough not to disturb him when he was in this mood, but was at the same time bursting to ventilate my reflections on this curious problem and hear how he would react to, and probably undermine, my hypotheses. Consequently, I sat myself in the armchair opposite, and reluctantly began to immerse myself in the recent novel of Gissing, which had been lying untouched on the side table since the day a few weeks ago when I purchased it. No shadow upon the quality of the book intended, I confess I must have fallen asleep while reading it, being somewhat fatigued by the day's peregrinations. When I woke up, the chair in front of me was empty, the only traces of its previous occupant being a blue dressing-gown carelessly slumped across its armrest and a pipe cast aside on the occasional table with a rapidity that had caused some of its ashes to fall out on the floor. I could read the signs and I knew what they meant, and subsequently I went to bed that night a solitary lodger.

I had barely fallen asleep, when I heard the sound of footsteps on the stairs outside. I gathered that it was Holmes returning from his nightly investigation, and fell back on my pillow, certain that he would retire to his bedroom and that the silence would be restored. But the sounds from within our sitting room did not die out, and I could hear him pacing up and down for a few minutes, before he came out onto the landing, climbed the stairs to my bedroom, and started to knock on my door.

"Watson? Watson! Are you asleep?"

I sighed and picked up my watch from the bedside table. It was only half past twelve. "Not quite," I replied.

"Excellent! I will be waiting for you in the sitting room. Make sure you wear your sturdy boots."

"Boots?" I said. "Do you mean to say that I should get dressed?"

But there was no answer. He had already gone back downstairs.

As one is wont to do when the promise of a good night's sleep is at hand, I quarrelled with myself for a moment, almost allowing fatigue to conquer over my curiosity and my wish to see the case through to the end. Already upon first hearing Holmes' voice outside the door, however, I had unconsciously decided to join him in the sitting room, and so within five minutes I was there, dressed in durable tweeds and, as instructed, sturdy boots. Holmes was still wearing his overcoat and gloves, and stood by the window as if keeping watch.

"Mycroft will be along shortly together with Mr Furniss. I believe we must go in the shelter of darkness if we want to draw this case to a satisfying conclusion."

"Where are we going?"

197

"Why, Rotherhithe, obviously. I just came back from there now, and sent word to Mycroft to come here with a four-wheeler."

"Why must we go back if you were just there?" I said, still a bit sulky from my rude awakening.

Holmes looked at me, his face betraying no thoughts. "Because they fly at night, Watson."

Two minutes later, a four-wheeler pulled up in front of the house, and we hurried down to embark upon the long journey to Rotherhithe. Mycroft looked less than pleased at being drawn out of the house at this late hour, and his young companion looked merely anxious, probably expecting this business to end in disaster.

"Holmes," I said impatiently, "will you let us know what you have been up to for the past few hours?"

"I have been to Rotherhithe. And I must commend you, Mr Furniss, upon your choice of tavern! They do serve an excellent cottage pie."

"Thank you, Mr Holmes," replied our client, "but what have you learned?"

Holmes' secretive smile only broadened.

"My friend Watson will tell you that it is a motto of mine that one must always eliminate every eventuality in a problem until one possibility remains, and that possibility, no matter how improbable, must be the truth. This case was essentially about time and distance. It was necessary for your enemies to bring the incriminating piece of evidence across the river in time for the police to discover it in their raid, and before you went to the banquet where your alibi would be indisputable. But the distance between the tavern where you gathered strength before the evening's social event and the low house in Wapping was much too great to transport the monocle from

198

one place to the other within the allotted time, and yet this plan was the one that your enemies thought the most efficient. They must therefore have had ready access to a method that made this plan possible before something simpler crossed their minds. I have spent the evening exploring the area between the tavern – which is located a few blocks from the banks of the Thames – and the river and I believe I have found the reason why your monocle made the journey across to Wapping without receiving any blemishes apart from a small fray on the cord."

"Ah, you noticed that too, did you, Sherlock?" said Mycroft. "Yes, it is evidently the trace of a—"

Holmes swiftly raised his forefinger to his lips. "It is better to show than to tell, don't you think, dear brother?"

Mycroft gently tapped the side of his nose and fell silent.

Holmes asked the driver to stop at a place where a long row of two-storey brick buildings lined the south bank of the river. We were now in an area that was both dark and foul-smelling, as a result of irregular street lights and mud-infested road surfaces, but I seemed to be the only member of our party who gave any thought to this. Furniss of course knew this district like the back of his hand, as did Holmes, and Mycroft looked rather more amused than vexed, as was his habit. Holmes led the way down a narrow passage lined with wooden hoardings until we came to the edge of the water, where the pebble beach sloped steeply down into the blackness. Here, Holmes halted and peered ahead towards something black and shapeless a few yards from the beach. To me, it looked like a small and primitive rowing boat. I thought the boat theory had been discarded, and was just about to say as much, when Holmes started pointing.

"There! Look!"

It was difficult to see anything at all in the darkness, but after a few seconds I could make out a silhouette that moved rapidly just above the surface of the water. It was apparently some sort of bird, flapping its wings so close to the water that it seemed to cause a few ripples now and then. As it neared the boat, a figure sitting in it raised an arm, and the bird promptly landed on it. Having shown us this curious spectacle, Holmes led us back up the passage again, not speaking until we were well out of earshot from the boat.

"I fail to see why we should observe a lone rower and his trained bird," I said.

"The reason is plain if you know something of the cultural history of China," said Holmes.

"China?"

Mycroft chuckled and placed a proud hand on the shoulder of his brother. "In China, fishing by way of trained cormorants is a practice dating back several centuries," he said. "It is still widespread on the country's many rivers, and according to tradition, it is best carried out at night. They tie a string around the neck of the bird so that, when it catches a fish, it will be unable to swallow it, thus carrying it back to the fisherman waiting in his boat. At the end of the procedure, the bird is rewarded by being allowed to swallow his final catch."

"Thank you for that concise lecture, dear brother," said Holmes, not altogether pleased at having been robbed of a portion of his performance. "I was not aware that the Chinese community of London had taken this custom with them from their native land, but now that I have seen it with my own eyes, it transpires as perfectly obvious. The London Chinese are mostly settled near the river in both Rotherhithe and Limehouse, and many of them lead a poor and squalid existence. Why not improve their lot in life by applying to the

Thames that knowledge which has been passed down through generations? The first clue to this was the frayed monocle cord, the fray being the clear trace of a bird's beak. Later when I wandered around the area this evening, I saw several Chinamen selling fish in the nearby market. I realised that this method was the only way of getting the monocle from the tavern to the brothel in so short a time."

"Good Heavens!" exclaimed Mr Furniss. "How improbable a solution!"

"And yet the truth," said Holmes.

"Shall we not arrest the man, then?"

Holmes raised his hand.

"That poor fisherman, I fear, if indeed he is the one, is only one link in a long and complicated chain. He lent his bird to the culprits, but we gain little by arresting him. Our next port of call must be the tavern!"

We continued through a maze of streets, leaving the river behind us. In due course, we came to a part of Rotherhithe where the streets were still peopled and groups of men and women congregated on street corners and in open doorways. At an intersection, we found the exterior of a public house where people were still at this late hour enjoying drinks and pouring out onto the pavement. A sign above the door bore the legend 'The Lighthouse' and showed a crude picture of a beacon lashed by furious seawaves. Holmes stepped into the taproom, and the landlord behind the counter smiled at our party. When he noticed Mr Furniss, he greeted him with hospitality, but there were also signs of unease in his face.

"The usual, Mr Furniss?" he tried.

It was Mycroft, who was obviously growing more and more impatient with his brother's drawn-out demonstration, who stepped up and shortened the process. "You have acted with dishonest intentions towards this man, sir. You or someone in your staff stole an object from him on Monday evening."

"I am sure I don't know what you are talking ab—"

"I am sure you do, my good man! We will be lenient with you if you assist us in our enquiries."

The man looked at us all in turn, his lower lip trembling increasingly. Finally, he surrendered, and confessed to having conspired against Mr Furniss. "But I swear to you, we had no intention to do so. A gentleman came and told us he would give us money if we acted according to his instructions. As we are a bit hard up at the moment, I accepted the offer, but when I heard who we were to deceive, I hesitated, knowing that Mr Furniss is a good and trusted customer. But I admit that the offer was too good to turn down."

Holmes stepped up to him. "I will do what I can to let off the hook, if you accompany us to the police to give them a full description of the man who instructed you, as I assume he did not give you a name."

The landlord consented after some persuading, and we were allowed to leave Rotherhithe to lay our case before the police. The rest of the investigation involved Holmes and me only indirectly, and unfortunately I am still prohibited from publicising the details of the case as we moved nearer to the identity of the brain behind the scheme. I can only say that it revealed forces within the corridors of Whitehall that any decent Englishman would probably prefer not to know about, and that Gregory Furniss turned out to have enemies more powerful and numerous than he could ever have suspected. Although the guilty parties were eventually put to justice, the experience proved much too daunting to a young and innocent man like Furniss, and he decided that his father's unfinished work in politics was best left to linger. What I can say is that an alleged connection between Furniss and a low house in Wapping never reached the papers, and that the man's future probably turned out happier for him than if he had pursued his career in politics, a career that I suspected he never really wanted for himself.

A few weeks after our excursion to Rotherhithe, we were paid a late-night visit by Mycroft at Baker Street, who joined Holmes and me by the fire with a cigar. Our conversation moved from one topic to another, until Mycroft brought up the business of trained cormorants.

"I must congratulate you, Sherlock, upon your triumph in the Furniss case, but since then, the details of that investigation have been at the back of my mind. To me, it seems likely that the men behind the plot to incriminate poor Furniss must have had a special connection with the cormorant trainers. They must have been known to them from the very start, when their plan took shape."

Holmes took the cigar from his mouth and glanced at his brother. "It is not unlikely that the Chinese fishermen have been used by the schemers in other affairs as well. In the days after our trip to Rotherhithe, that query gnawed away at me too, and so I consulted my commonplace books for possible links with other cases. I found at least four thefts that had taken place near the river in that part of London, all of them involving pieces of jewellery being snatched from someone's person in the dark of the night. But the most interesting eventuality was the link with the disappearance of the Ferrers documents three months ago, which would indicate that a trained cormorant was employed by political conspirators already at that date."

"Sounds to me like a case of a thieving magpie!" I said.

"Yes," said Holmes, "but one with a slightly more refined taste."

Also from Peter Andersson

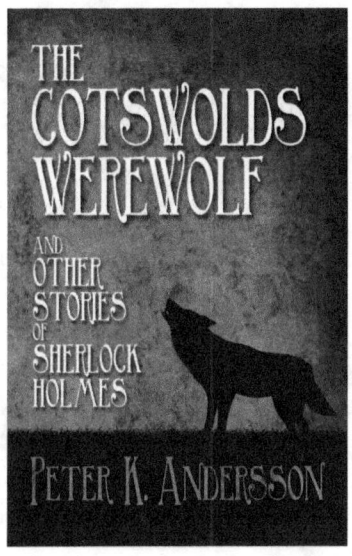

The Cotswolds Werewolf
and Other Stories of Sherlock Holmes

Someone is killing sheep in the Cotswolds. Or something. As
Holmes and Watson arrive in the tranquility of a little village
of shepherds and farmers to enjoy a few restful days in the
idyllic countryside, strange things start to occur.

This volume also includes four shorter stories in the vein of
Conan Doyle: 'The Adventure of the Velvet Lampshade', 'The
Adventure of the Missing Mudlark', 'The Adventure of the
Forking Paths', and 'The Adventure of the One-Armed Pugilist'.

Also from MX Publishing

MX Publishing is the world's largest specialist Sherlock Holmes publisher, with over a hundred titles and fifty authors creating the latest in Sherlock Holmes fiction and non-fiction.

From traditional short stories and novels to travel guides and quiz books, MX Publishing cater for all Holmes fans.

The collection includes leading titles such as *Benedict Cumberbatch In Transition* and *The Norwood Author* which won the 2011 Howlett Award (Sherlock Holmes Book of the Year).

MX Publishing also has one of the largest communities of Holmes fans on Facebook with regular contributions from dozens of authors.

www.mxpublishing.com

Also from MX Publishing

Our bestselling books are our short story collections;

'Lost Stories of Sherlock Holmes, 'The Outstanding Mysteries of Sherlock Holmes, The Papers of Sherlock Holmes Volume 1 and 2, 'Untold Adventures of Sherlock Holmes (and the sequel 'Studies in Legacy) and 'Sherlock Holmes in Pursuit', 'The Cotswold Werewolf and Other Stories of Sherlock Holmes – and many more……

www.mxpublishing.com